The
Counterfeits

The Counterfeits

GOOD GIRLS WITH BAD GIRL TENDENCIES

Kierra Smith

THE COUNTERFEITS
GOOD GIRLS WITH BAD GIRL TENDENCIES

iUniverse books may be ordered through booksellers or by contacting:

iUniverse
1663 Liberty Drive
Bloomington, IN 47403
www.iuniverse.com
1-800-Authors (1-800-288-4677)

ISBN: 978-1-4917-9136-3 (sc)
ISBN: 978-1-4917-9137-0 (e)

Library of Congress Control Number: 2016903199

Print information available on the last page.

iUniverse rev. date: 03/03/2016

ACKNOWLEDGMENTS

This book is dedicated to my sisters:

*L*aJuana M.is my oldest sister. She's extremely sophisticated, but no one knows that there is a daredevil that comes out to play every now and then and just like the rest of us, she gets in trouble.

LaKenya B. is the sweet and charming sister, but if you're not careful you'll miss that she's stuck her claws in you and escaping is no longer an option.

Kennesha S. is the youngest, but she swears that she's the oldest sister. The other sisters have learned so much from her adventurous life. Her hap-hazardous lifestyle keeps us all on guard because we never know when we'll have to come to her rescue.

Tiana W. has been a friend for almost two decades and the sisters consider her as one of their own. She's also known as the peace-maker, but her inability to tolerate foolishness has the tendency to have us all sitting in jail, pleading our case. (Who is "Emma"?).

And to my other sisters and friends who also mean so much to me, you all help in keeping me grounded. You all have been an ear and/or shoulder in some of my darkest moments and I thank you:

Rocenia A., Kelita B., DeAnna B., Jasmine B., Patrice D., Cushanna D., Ariesha D., Randi E., Zshawntinique E.,

Yolanda H., Shaloea H., Ashley K., Marnasha J., Trarie J., Sha- Nail J., Donna L., Valerie M., Ashley M., Dietrice M., Kristi M., Celeste M., Allysia P., Kelley R., Ashely R., Goldie S., Charisse T., Michell T., Zainab T., Kiyana W., Danielle W., Stephanie W., Monee W., Destiny W., Crystal W., Kiara W., Tiffany W.

If I forgot anyone, please charge it to my head and not my heart, I love you all.

I'd lastly like to thank my husband for his patience during my writing sessions. Often times I neglect him while trying to get my thoughts onto paper, but I ALWAYS make it up to him. **Don't I, Big Daddy?**

Now for the moment that you've all been waiting for...

BOOK 1

CCW & The Game Changer

"Recap"

THE SISTERS

*W*aking the next morning, Carla glanced at her phone, she didn't have any missed calls or any awaiting text messages. For somebody who needed her two days ago, Joshua was sure acting as if he didn't know her now. But, she wouldn't jump to conclusions; he hadn't returned his daughters' calls either.

Carla saw Jasmine and Jayla off to their cars, hoping that she would see them again in the near future. Carla stretched across her bed, trying not to be edgy when the Rick Ross ring tone began playing again. The irritation that had consumed her all morning was held at bay when she answered to see what her sister wanted.

"Hey Bay Bay!" Carla cheered as she tried to camouflage how she actually felt at that moment.

"Why does it sound like you just ran over your dog?" Chrissey inquired, bypassing the falsetto.

Laughing at Chrissey's inability to be tactful, "I don't know, I'm alright, what's up with you?"

Evading her question, Chrissey continued, "What do you have up your sleeve this weekend?"

"I don't have any plans at the moment. I thought about coming home, but I don't know!"

"Aww, Yaay, okay we're on our way!"

"Huh? Who?" Carla's excitement escalated.

"Ebony, Morgan and I are on the road, we will be there in about two hours. We're about to pave the streets of downtown Chicago, it's going down sis!"

Smiling with tears in her eyes, "I can't wait, I'll text you the address of the hotel." Pausing at the thought. "I can't wait to see you guys!" Carla added again.

At that moment, Carla said a silent prayer of thanks to God. No matter how far she strayed away from him, she was more than confident that God never left her side. No one could convince her that he hadn't sent her sisters to her rescue and for that she was grateful.

When the knock came at the door two and half hours later, Carla didn't have to guess who the guests were. Swinging open the door, she found her three favorite people standing at her threshold. Jumping on them and throwing her arms around all three before they could come inside, she squealed at the top of her lungs. "God, I missed y'all!"

"Damn Bay Bay, you acting like you won the lottery or something!" Chrissey couldn't help but observe.

"Your ass is ignorant, dude. I just needed y'all, that's all." Carla's motto was: *you didn't need friends when you had sisters.*

"Where is that nice piece of ass that you brought home?" Chrissey asked, looking around the room.

Morgan chimed in, "Damn Chrissey, you're going to get us put out and we've only been here five minutes."

"Thanks Morgan, Chrissey acts like she doesn't have any home training." Carla rolled her eyes.

"I was only joking." Morgan laughed. "Where is that nice piece of ass that I know has spread you like an eagle by now?"

"Ebony please tell me that you have some kind of sense unlike the other stooges?" Carla ignored Morgan and turned towards her oldest sister.

"Hell naw, I'm just as ignorant as they are. We need to know if the man gave you some act right. The way your mood swings were set up, we thought about selling you like Joseph and the coat of many colors from the bible."

Carla laughed because she knew she was a piece of work, but she couldn't have been that bad. "Ha. Whatever. So what do you guys want to do first?"

Picking up on the fact that Carla eluded the question, Morgan helped her switch the subject. "I think that we could just call it a girl's night in today because it's getting late and we just got off the road." Flipping through the yellow pages that were on the countertop, she had an idea. "I think pizza, chicken, drinks, and a chick flick are in order."

With a little bit of wine in their systems and a belly full of Chicago Style Pizza, the open forum began with Morgan. "So, I don't think I want to be married!"

The room was silent and she had everyone's attention, so Morgan carried on. "I don't think I want that kind of commitment anymore. The relationship I have with Brandon is tired, repetitive and unfulfilling." Inhaling a mouthful of air and going in for the kill, "I think I want to test the waters a little bit more!" Morgan confessed.

"What the hell does testing the waters consist of?" Carla couldn't resist asking.

"This discussion is not about interrogation Carla, just let her speak her piece. You got married before you were completely ready and look what happened!" Chrissey exclaimed.

"Uh hold on hoe ---." Carla went to defend herself and Ebony cut her off.

"Ivan can't have kids!"

"Whhhat?" Everyone chorused.

There was an unspoken rule that no one ever mentioned the fact that Amber was not Ivan's biological daughter. He had been there for Ebony and Amber in ways that most biological fathers weren't in traditional households.

"So what are you guys going to do?" Chrissey asked first.

"I thought you said no interrogation?" Carla corrected.

Cutting her eyes at Carla was Chrissey's only response.

Pausing to gather the strength Carla needed to come clean, since she was the next one to share. "Yes, I screwed the old man and he went out of town yesterday and I haven't heard from him since."

It seemed as if there was more than three pair of eyes on her. "And I swallowed!"

Chrissey broke the silence with giggles. "That's my girl; I knew I taught you better than that patty cake shit you were doing with Dre!"

Rolling her eyes in response to Chrissey's amusement. "Okay, so what news do you have to reveal?" Carla diverted her attention solely to Chrissey.

Tapping the tip of her chin, "I'm still getting laid on a regular basis. I still don't do commitments. I don't want to get married. Oh and we all know that I'm not having any children." Chrissey looked around. "Yep, everything's still the same with me!"

"You're ignorant dude." Morgan told Chrissey with a gurgle.

"Carla, there is one other thing." Chrissey pointed her finger in the air to give the impression that she remembered her thought. "I got a speeding ticket and I had to use your name because you know my license is still suspended."

Everyone laughed, except Carla. "That shit isn't funny, I'm going to kill you Chrissey, damn man!" Launching in her direction, Chrissey took off running around the room in an attempt to escape Carla's wrath. No one knew better than Chrissey that her sister was capable of bodily harm and since the age of ten, she tested the theory to no end. Chrissey had more bruises and scratches from Carla than she accumulated through her past life of a tomboy.

Fast- forward five months

*O*pening the front door, their eyes connected and Carla found her voice. "What are you doing here?"

Moving towards the opening of the door, Joshua explained, "I didn't want to wait until tomorrow; I think I've harbored this long enough."

Carla felt her temper slowly rising from the weight of the last five months and all that she had endured. "You didn't seem to give two shits a few months ago; it didn't stop you from blocking me on Facebook and Twitter. Or, ordering your service provider to restrict your phone from receiving incoming calls and then ultimately disconnecting the line altogether."

"There were just some things that I couldn't explain at the time and I couldn't deal with you and all of the other circumstances that I had going on!" He tried to explain.

"You mean like that baby?" Carla questioned.

With his face hardening, he took a few minutes to adjust. Joshua had come to Michigan to lay his burdens at her feet, but somehow Carla already knew. "Huh?" Joshua asked pretending to be confused.

"Please don't fucking play with me, I'm so ready to fight you!" Carla warned.

"Okay, so you know about my daughter!" Joshua confirmed.

"Know about your daughter? Nicca I know about all of your kids and the poor excuse of a father that you were."

"Excuse you?" Joshua stepped closer, there was a thin line that Carla had visibly crossed.

"You're excused. Who did you think I was? Did you expect me to sit around and wait for you to give me closure - wait for you to fill the hole that you left?" Carla didn't give him an opportunity to chime in or explain. "You should have known better! I told you what I was capable of, how I operated once I was determined to get answers." Carla waved her arms in the air to get her point across. "I refuse to be a victim to men that think their actions have no repercussions. I'm sure you thought you were in the clear because I was silent!"

"You're right I should have known better than to fucking make a deal with the devil on a chick like you, then crawl into your bed with a false expectation that I could walk away feeling nothing!"

"Whoa, make a deal with the devil on me?" Carla paused.

"Listen little girl, I was a player way before I became a grown man, I told you that. And there is no way that I don't get what I want, but I didn't count on loving you. I didn't count on opening up to you."

"Bullshit! Tell me about the deal?" Carla spat.

"That shit doesn't matter CeCe!" The slither in his tongue dialed down a bit. Joshua hadn't meant to mention the bet, but she roiled him up and he lost control.

She watched him step back so she came out of the door and stood on the porch. "No it matters, you were talking big shit minutes ago, don't back down now."

"Girl, you know what…?" Joshua began walking towards the stairs to leave.

Noticing that Joshua had dismissed her without another word, she figured she ought to go for the juggler. "Go ahead and leave, that's what you're good at, that's what you do, that's who you ---."

Joshua had turned around, raced back up the steps and pushed her into the front door, snatching the words out of her mouth. "Do you think I wanted to leave you? Do you? Do you think after making love with you, burying my secrets and fears inside of you that I wanted to leave you, Carla? That I wanted to walk away with the risk that you wouldn't be here when I came back?"

Standing there silent and numb, Carla was trying to gather her thoughts, but her mind was whirling. She wanted to be pissed, she wanted to be upset, but something inside of her just couldn't. So she listened to him explain.

Moving into the house and sitting on the couch to resume the speech Joshua had been practicing for weeks. "Sug, I left to go back to Pennsylvania because my ex's sister, Breanne, came to visit me." Pausing to let the first piece of information settle in. "Do you remember the week you insisted that I was being weird? She showed up the night that I cancelled our date." Joshua took a deep breath. "Supposedly, my ex-girlfriend waited until the end of her pregnancy to tell me that she'd gotten pregnant before we broke up. She wanted to be sure that she would be able to carry the baby because at thirty-nine years of age, she was considered high risk. I left to attend the baby shower and to talk to her."

"You're talking about Vanessa?" Carla tried to get clarity.

Joshua was a man who respected his privacy as well as others, and part of the reason why he didn't open up to people was because he didn't deal in exchanging information. "How do you know her name? Who are you Google Williams now?"

Carla squared her shoulders and crouched down so that they were eye-level since Joshua remained seated. "Who do you think hacked into your Facebook account? It for damn sure wasn't the FBI or the CIA."

Leaning back on the sofa, Joshua rubbed his hand over his beard as he recalled the twenty-four hour time frame that he was locked out of his Gmail and Facebook account. "You do understand that it's a federal offense to enter into someone's email?"

"I know what the fuck it is, but it should also be a crime to walk out on someone who loves you. Leaving them crying and sobbing because the hurt and pain cuts deep and without any reasoning or explanation, just speculation. While you went on, not giving a fuck if they lived or died, you ignored the begging and pleading that was left on your voicemail. Not to mention the unanswered calls and text messages that date back as far as the day you left."

"So excuse me if I lost it." Carla continued, "I was irrational in my attempts to find a resolution. But, if you could feel the hurt and pain that I carried around for months wondering what I had done for you to leave me, maybe you could sympathize. I went through every moment and memory that I had of you, trying to pinpoint where we went wrong. Contemplating if you were real or if I had conjured you up!" Carla sobbed.

Joshua didn't know what to think of the situation that money and greed had placed him in, but he had no choice but to give her the truth and see what it afforded him. "Do you know what your husband does for a living?"

"Ex- husband." She corrected.

"Since when?" He posed.

"Since you left!" She confirmed. "I thought about re-considering once I saw that you had fathered another baby, but it didn't make me love you any less."

Rubbing the temples of his head, Joshua felt that Carla was making this harder than it needed to be. Love made this harder than it had to be. "We buried the baby four months ago, Sug." It didn't matter how many times he said it or tried to push his baby girl to the back of his mind, the pain was still present.

"What do you mean you buried her?" Carla asked confused.

"The Baby Shower never took place because by the time I got to Vanessa, she had been rushed to the hospital and prepped for an emergency C- Section. The baby lived a couple days before her heart gave out. She had a Ventricular Septal Defect (VSD)."

Looking at the puzzled expression on Carla's face, Joshua elaborated. "It's a large hole in the heart where the blood does not flow properly through the body. The doctors weren't able to detect it and it caused heart failure accompanied with the fact that she wasn't full term yet."

The silence had begun to consume her, she had to say something. "Babe, I don't know what to say. I honestly couldn't image how you or Vanessa feel!" Joining him on the couch, Carla encircled her arms around him. She wasn't disappointed when Joshua returned the hug and buried his face in the crook of her neck as he had done many times before. But, the sentimental moment dissolved when Joshua's hand began to travel up and down her body.

"Please don't do that!" Carla tried to grab his hand as the desire raised in her throat, causing her to be out of breath.

Joshua inhaled her scent. "You have no idea how much I've missed you, craved you." Lifting his head with his eyes fixed on her lips.

In a perfect world Carla didn't have a right to ask or inquire about what he conducted outside of her presence, but she couldn't help the tinge of jealousy that surfaced at the thought.

"I need to know if you used your well endowed, God-gifted anatomy to console Vanessa?"

Extracting his hand from around her waist, Joshua looked at Carla as if she had lost her mind. "Did I come in here questioning you about who you've been with?" Joshua asked defensively.

"No, but it wouldn't matter because I haven't been with anyone! So your question and the discussion would have been moot."

"That's a lie and you know it!" Joshua charged.

Turning her face in disgust. "Do I look like a whore to you?"

Joshua jumped off the couch to distance himself. "I hear what your mouth is saying, but your ass and hips are much wider than they were the last time I was inside of you. Nothing, but some dick has you spread out like that because a dildo doesn't stand a chance." Joshua insulted.

Instantaneously, all of the blood drained from Carla's face, replacing it with pure fire! She couldn't decide if she should be the bigger person and escort Joshua to the door. Or, excuse herself to go in search of her gun and wear his rude ass out with the butt of it. Carla hadn't been to the gun range in months and she was dying to relieve some stress.

Instead of resulting to violence, Carla was going to use a different approach. She moved off of the couch and closed the distance between them. She reached for both of

Joshua's hands and placed one on each side of her hips. With softened eyes, she whispered so calmly that it shook her. "My hips have spread because the seed that you left inside of me refuses to stop growing!"

Snatching his hands and stepping back with a quiet storm broiling in his eyes. "That's some low shit for you to claim to be pregnant, knowing that I just buried a child."

"Do you honestly believe that I would lie about a baby?"

"Carla you would have to be at least five months pregnant!"

Amused with his quick calculations, Carla reaffirmed. "I am five months pregnant Daddy and it's a boy!"

Joshua's fury escalated. "You aren't pregnant and you for damn sure aren't five months, I know what five months pregnant looks like."

"Excuse you? Are you trying to intentionally piss me off? Are you trying to make me blow this bitch up with you still in it?" Carla raged.

"There's no way in hell that I'm raising another son! So I don't know what you're going to do. I made a promise to myself not to have any more children, let alone another son." Joshua informed her.

Yelling at the top of her lungs, "Got dammit, you don't get to make gender calls and if you would keep your dick in your pants, I assure you that these little bald headed ass babies would stop surfacing."

Carla hadn't noticed the deadliness that Joshua possessed in his walk before, but she stood her ground. "You're walking on thin ice baby girl, so I would tread lightly if I were you."

Carla had never been the one to take threats lightly and she was the rowdiest out of all of her sisters. At the moment, she was more than hormonal, she was livid with Joshua. But, she knew that this next gut punch would have to be rendered as subtle as possible. "Just because your son Jonathan has identity issues doesn't mean that my son will."

"What the fuck did you just say?" Joshua questioned harshly.

Carla exhaled. "I know that he likes to wear women's clothing." Pausing to gather her thoughts and to give Joshua a chance to stop her, but he didn't, so she continued. "I also know that he wears wigs, sew-in's and make-up. From my understanding of the description, Jonathan is a drag queen, a transvestite!"

Joshua balled up his fist while trying to calm his composure, but failing with every attempt. He grabbed the nearest ornament that decorated Carla's coffee table and threw it against the wall. With every bit of anger that he could muster, it left a hole the size of his hand as the evidence. "Do you know what pisses me off the most about you?" He peddled forward without any indication that he expected her to answer the question.

"You found the time to dig into every aspect of my life, but you are oblivious and naïve about the bullshit that's right under your nose. You married a man and had no clue of the pull or power that he possessed. So tell me, did your nosey ass know that your husband hired me to distract you, to pull you in and then leave you? Dre wanted you back so bad that he paid me half of a million dollars to ensure that you would return back to him as damaged goods! He wanted the break to be so detrimental that you wouldn't be able to function without him and he could be the one to mend and nurse you back to health."

"What? That doesn't even make sense. He didn't know anything about the merger or even that our paths would cross!" Carla informed Joshua.

"For you to be so intelligent, you are quite adolescent. He headed the damn merger; he owns shares in the corporation that you work for. Dre approached me way before there was any talk of a merger."

Numb to the revelation, Carla calmly asked. "So who are you? Do you actually work for the corporation or is this all a scam?"

"I'm known as Ice!"

"What is that, an acronym?"

"No. It's a name that I adopted because of my ability to be cold, unattached, and unaffected by anyone or anything. Until I met you."

"Sounds heartless." Carla bypassed his last confession.

"It's smart, that's what it is. I have never fallen for an assignment in the active fifteen years of this occupation."

Closing her eyes to stop her hands from shaking, Carla asked, "And what exactly is your occupation?"

"I'm currently the head trainer at your bank, but in my past life I was a male escort." Joshua admitted.

"You mean a male prostitute?" Carla corrected.

"No, I said a male escort."

"Please elaborate on what the difference is between the two." Carla crossed her legs and interlocked her arms.

"The difference is that I don't stand on a corner, strung out on drugs with my dick in my hand."

"If this was about an assignment and money, then why fuck me? You could have done your job without including sex."

"I slept with you because he doesn't deserve you! And at the time, I needed you."

"Excuse me? But, you deserve me?"

"No, I don't deserve you either. But, I could have stayed in Pennsylvania with Vanessa. I came back for you. I loved you enough to be monogamous in the bedroom unlike your husband."

Sitting back on the cushions of the couch, she was trying to find comfort as the baby began to push down on her bladder. "Was that a cheap shot?" Carla registered.

"No Carla, it was the truth! He doesn't respect you and he doesn't really want you. But, he understands your value and doesn't want anyone else to have you."

Rolling her eyes in the top of her head, Carla tried to clarify. "Hmm, more of your psychology? So, let me guess. You guys discussed this over tea while you were planning on how to strategically seduce and deceive me?"

"No I concluded this when I realized that my daughter Jasmine orchestrated this scheme. And then again, when Jasmine revealed that Dre was the father of her unborn child."

Stunned at the revelation. Carla began to think back on her initial encounter with Jasmine at her hotel room in Chicago and the baby bump that she noticed shortly after the introductions.

Propping up on the sofa, Carla felt a wave of nausea sweep over her. She couldn't help but think of how dysfunctional this whole situation was. And now she had this life growing inside of her and its Daddy was some kind of player/pimp/hoe. Along with his daughter, who was just as manipulative and deceptive as Joshua.

When realization dawned on Carla that she wasn't going to be able to contain the contents of her stomach, she went in search of the bathroom. Just as she opened the lid of the toilet, the vomit spilled into the water. The wrenching became so intense that it brought her to her knees and blinded her eyes with tears. Carla hadn't noticed that Joshua entered the bathroom, let alone that he kneeled down behind her and wrapped his arms around her stomach to hold her and the baby.

Carla rested her head on the toilet seat and Joshua leaned his head on the side of her temple enough for his lips to touch her ears and whispered, "I'm here Baby, you're not alone." Joshua exhaled a sigh of relief as the weight of his secrets had been released. "You can count on me; we'll figure it out together." Joshua reassured.

Stifling tears and trying to wipe the snot from her nose, Carla clearly recited her feelings. "I, nor this baby need you, please leave!" Carla didn't have the strength to fight or to yell anymore and she wasn't going to put her pregnancy at risk to do so.

Feeling the baby move underneath his fingers for the first time, Joshua made a decision. "I'm not leaving now Carla, it's too late. Don't you get what happened? This was never supposed to be!" Joshua tightened his grip on her waistline. "I wasn't supposed to love you and you weren't supposed to dig into my life and tear down every wall that I've built." He placed his nose in the crook of her neck. "You divorced Dre instead of going back to him. He's not just going to let that go. There are repercussions for that and I won't put you or this baby in anymore danger." Joshua took a deep breath and mumbled, "Sug, we've officially changed the game."

Welcome to the Sequel:

The Counterfeits

GOOD GIRLS WITH BAD GIRL TENDENCIES

"Sister. She is your mirror, shining back at you with a world of possibilities. She is your witness, who sees you at your worst and best, and loves you anyway. She is your partner in crime, your midnight comp\anion, someone who knows when you are smiling, even in the dark. She is your teacher, your defense attorney, your personal press agent, even your shrink. Some days, she's the reason you wish you were an only child."

-**Barbara Alpert**

CHAPTER 1

When 2 Or 3 Are Gathered Together...

The way that indecision hung in the air, one would have thought that Chrissey was staring down the barrel of a gun. But, it was much simpler than that as she watched her male companion check into the Westin Hotel with his side-piece.

Chrissey's first thought was to just set the car on fire with the emergency gasoline that she kept in her trunk. If she had to bet on this situation, she would deem it as a crisis. For the first time in her life, she was at a cross-road and she needed a little assistance. She backed in between the bushes near the entrance, pulled her cell phone out of her pocket and dialed the sister that was closest to her location.

When the connection broke in the line, Chrissey heard the sleep lingering in Carla's voice. "Hello?" When Carla didn't get a response, she repeated herself. "Hello?"

"Oh sorry Carla, I got distracted." Chrissey answered.

Carla breathed a sigh of relief. "What's going on, Pooty?"

Chrissey paused. "I think we should set his car on fire!"

Lifting her body out of the bed, Carla needed to ensure that she heard Chrissey correctly. "Who? Set whose car on fire?"

"Daniel's car!" Chrissey whispered.

"Oh My God, where are you?" Carla had gotten out of bed and began moving around to find some clothes that she could actually fit.

"At the Westin Hotel, right here on Ten Mile right passed Evergreen." She informed.

"Okay Chrissey, well wait a damn minute, let me call Morgan and Ebony!"

"Ugh, are you trying to incriminate all of us?" Chrissey asked.

"Dude, I'm not going to jail by myself! Are you trying to send me into premature labor?" Carla was an octave just above yelling.

"Okay, Okay, Okay, just hurry up. I can't keep hiding in these bushes!" Chrissey urged as she disconnected the call.

Carla looked at the phone as the line went dead. "Bushes? This girl has completely gone off the deep end!" Tapping the phone icon on her Note 3, she called Morgan and then Ebony as she slipped on her shoes and grabbed her jacket.

Ten minutes later, Chrissey watched as Carla's Jeep pulled into the parking lot, followed by Ebony's and then Morgan's. Chrissey figured it was safe to come out of hiding when her phone chimed and Carla asked the location of the bush that she hid under.

Stepping out front and sprinting towards her sisters and Morgan, who was more like a sister rather than Carla's best-friend, Chrissey greeted them. "Punta's, hug my neck."

"Where is your car?" Ebony questioned, looking around to observe her surroundings.

"I switched cars with Tasha. Hello, I couldn't do a following detail in my own automobile." Tasha was Chrissey's Morgan. Although they hadn't been friends as long as Carla and Morgan had, Chrissey definitely considered Tasha to be a rider.

"So what the hell is going on?" Morgan butted in.

"Daniel and his troll just went into the hotel." Chrissey pointed towards the entrance of the hotel before returning her attention back to her sisters. " I think we should set his car on fire!"

"Whoa, Arson is not going to look good on my record. You know I just got that one thing cleared." Ebony spread her legs and folded her arms above her head. When she rocked back and forth, her sisters knew that she was thinking. Ebony considered it to be a strategizing method while they just believed she had a nervous condition.

"Can we just paint the car a different color? I mean it's white, so we can paint it any color!" Carla suggested.

"Or we could puncture every tire and leave a few eggs on the windshield!" Morgan countered.

"I like that!" Carla agreed with Morgan. "But only puncture three tires."

Morgan was half confused and half curious. "Why only three tires?"

"Because the insurance company will repair it if all four tires are flat. Only flattening three will guarantee he'll be screwed." Carla explained.

"Listen, I want to torch his shit! I want his cheating ass to walk home!" Chrissey was fuming and she could feel the steam seeping from her pores. She was tired of listening to them rationalize explanations, she meant business and she was ready to prove it.

"Whatever we do, we can't keep standing here. I'm sure there is a camera somewhere watching our every move as we stand here plotting." Carla announced. The truth was that she was the nervous one; she kept her dirt to a minimum because she refused to do jail time. At the age of fifteen, her mother Eileen noticed the temper that she hid so well.

Eileen had told her that if she ever went to jail because of her inability to control her rage, she would leave her there regardless of the amount of bail.

"Well the way your stomach has expanded, hiding you is not an option at this point and time." Morgan rubbed Carla's protruding stomach.

"I see your bald-headed ass got jokes. It's 2am and you got fat people jokes." Carla moved her stomach out of Morgan's reach.

"Aww, come here big girl, don't be offended. Pregnancy agrees with you, you had five months of just hips and booty and now you have a little bit of belly." Morgan tried to hug Carla.

Shit, Carla was just thankful that her stomach had finally rounded and she didn't just look overweight anymore.

"Can y'all two fruit cakes stay focused?" Chrissey raised her hand in the air to get their attention.

"I'll take a Vandalism charge over Arson." Ebony interjected.

"Ok, I have a can of red paint in the car!" Chrissey obliged.

"So, you're a carpenter now?" Ebony asked jokingly.

Chrissey's only reply was a smirk. No one knew that she had been planning this heist for weeks. Daniel wasn't her boyfriend per se, but she didn't believe in community dick because she didn't walk around making public announcements about free coochie.

While they worked effortlessly, yet efficiently, Morgan extracted her pocket knife in and out of the three tires. Ebony teepee'd the car with tissue and napkins from her glove compartment that stuck nicely to the smashed egg yolks that Carla's hungry ass provided.

Of course, Chrissey wasn't going to be out-done by her creative sisters. She painted the word **'Dirty'** on the right side of the car and the word **'Dick'** on the left side. Once they were satisfied with their handiwork, all four girls slipped behind the wheels of their vehicles with an agreement to meet for lunch once everyone got some sleep.

Chapter 2

The Aftermath.

The ladies slid into the booth at Bar 7 in Southfield, which had become their safe haven. In the sacredness of their reserved booth, they talked about their problems, fears and their men. When the sisters called a meeting, nothing was off-limits for discussion.

Chrissey was the last one to sit at the table because she was late as usual. "Did you guys order yet? I'm starving!"

"I ordered chicken wings!" Carla spoke first.

"I ordered spinach dip." Ebony countered.

"And I ordered the hamburger sliders." Morgan confirmed.

"Good, I'll get the cajun chicken and shrimp pasta." Chrissey settled.

"Sooooooo, Chrissey could you be so kind to explain to us, why in the hell we did that to that man's Challenger? When in fact, you don't have a commitment with him nor do you want one!" Carla sparked the conversation because she had done some thinking in her spare time. Her hormones hadn't allowed her to think before speaking and although she couldn't undo the damage that was done, she still needed an explanation of some sort.

"Carla, it's the principle! Would you allow Joshua to go off and be with another woman without consequences?"

Chrissey confronted Carla, knowing the answer before she spoke it.

"Uh lil crazy? I'm having his baby and we are cohabitating. Joshua can't go to the bathroom without me getting suspicious. There is no way that he would make it to a hotel room without me body bagging his ass first."

"Exactly!" Chrissey threw her hands in the air. Point made, she rested her case.

"But, Chrissey you said out of your own mouth that you don't do relationships or commitments. So why be so crazy?" Morgan asked.

"Because I like him!" Chrissey exclaimed.

"Don't tell me we just did all that shit because she "*likes*" him!" Ebony's irritation was growing. She was the oldest and she prided herself on not publicly responding to foolishness, but somehow she always found herself bending her rules for the exception of her sisters. Yet, the more Chrissey talked, the more Ebony began rethinking this silent loyalty pact.

"This clown just made us her puppets!" Morgan laughed hysterically, nothing Chrissey said or did seemed to surprise her. She loved her like a sister and admired her spunk.

"How long have you been messing with Daniel, Chrissey?" Carla was trying to mentally calculate.

"Off and on for three years! Sometimes he's here, sometimes he disappears." Chrissey admitted.

"Okay well until your twenty-six year old ass grows up enough to admit that you have deeper feelings for him, don't call my pregnant ass any more unless it's a damn emergency." Carla scolded.

"Agreed." Morgan chimed.

"Agreed." Ebony reaffirmed.

"Fine!" Chrissey wasn't offended because she could have easily pulled the heist off without their help. But, since her sisters seemed to be a little pissed off, she decided to hold that piece of truth.

"And just so we're clear," Carla added. "Emergencies are incidents that involve blood, tragedies that are death related and crimes that accompany jail time!"

Everyone laughed at Carla's inability to be subtle with her explanation. She had a way with words that either made you laugh or pissed you off.

For the remainder of the meal, casual conversation floated over and around Chrissey, but she wasn't paying much attention to any of it. Yet, she gave the expected responses of, *oh okay, yeah, really? Get out? Shut up, you're kidding.* Chrissey had dated enough men that she knew how to play along, however she was reflecting on what her sisters had said. And although it stung a bit, Chrissey could respect it as the truth.

Maybe Daniel felt that he hadn't owed her anything because of the label or the lack thereof on their relationship. But, it was in Chrissey's experience that you couldn't trust men of Daniel's caliber because the only woman that governed their hearts, were the "Almighty Dollar".

She had been in the game long enough to understand that a man loved his money more than his woman and if he cared about a woman then he spent his money on her. Maybe that was why the hotel scene had gotten to her so badly. If Daniel was willing to treat the side-piece to the Westin, then that meant she wasn't a Motel 6 kind of tramp. When men start upgrading hoes to hospitality suites, then you have a problem.

Chrissey understood what men wanted from women, so she used it to her advantage. Instead of being a doormat or a storage bucket for a man's cum, she observed and acquired the technique to play the game. It was second nature to her, as if it had been boiled in with her DNA. Some men were offended by how knowledgeable she was when it came to the opposite sex, but that was a personal problem for them. It had only taken Chrissey one time to be burned and she vowed that it wouldn't happen again.

Men wanted sex and she wanted security, which ultimately equaled money. The way she figured it, she hadn't strayed too far from God because the bible even acknowledged that money answered all things. And since the men were calling, she didn't mind answering as long as money was on the other end of the connection.

Chrissey's logic didn't make her money hungry and it for damn sure didn't make her a hoe. She understood that you could get what you wanted from a man without ever spreading your legs. Her mother Eileen had continuously stressed how valuable your vagina was and the price that it held. Eileen would say, *"THIS IS GOLD, IF A MAN LOVES YOU, HE WILL MARRY YOU TO UNCOVER THE TREASURE."*

Chrissey agreed with her mother's logic to a certain extent, but her bills weren't going to pay themselves based on gold and treasure. Chrissey had fallen in love with money at the age of sixteen; she wasn't sure where the fascination had surfaced from. But, the desire for wanting to look good had sprouted right around the time that her breast had blossomed from a bird's chest to a bird's nest.

Her sisters were content with having clothes that looked cute, but she wouldn't settle until every piece of clothing and every matching accessory that adorned her closest was labeled with a high-end designer attached to it. Nonetheless, she tried to be discreet with her fetish because the names and brands weren't for others, they were for her. Unless someone actually read the label hidden inside the material, they would assume the clothing was expensive. Looking at the label, conveyed just how pricey it was. Material seemed to feel different when it was authentic and designed by names that were hard to find and even harder to pronounce.

Paying the bill and departing from her sister's approximately two hours later, Chrissey figured that she might as well stop by Daniel's house and check on him. She couldn't help laughing to herself. *What had his face looked like when he checked out of the hotel this morning?* Chrissey was sure that he was embarrassed and possibly humiliated, but he would think that next time he wanted to step out.

Chrissey had been with Daniel out of convenience initially, but if she were honest with herself, she cared more than she led on. Unfortunately, voicing those feelings would cost her more than she was willing to risk.

As she pulled into the driveway of Daniel's condo off Northwestern Highway, Chrissey put the car in park behind the vandalized Challenger muscle car. She exhaled, gearing herself for the fight of her life. She demanded respect and if she had to tear up all of his shit until she got it then that's exactly what she was prepared to do.

Instead of using her key, Chrissey decided that it was best to knock first. She wasn't willing to walk into the house blind-sided.

Everything was so quiet inside; her feet automatically began shuffling because her nerves were on edge. Chrissey saw the car and assumed that Daniel was in the house, but she didn't hear his body toddling to get to the door, so maybe he wasn't. Just as she was about to insert her key in the door, the knob turned and slowly screeched open.

Looking at the figure that hid in the shadows, she noticed that his 9 mm hung loosely in his left hand. Not sure if she should run or scream, she slowly began backing away from the door, when he called out. "Hell naw, you better get your ass in this house, Chrissey."

With her hands in a surrendering stance, Chrissey replied, "You know Babe, I don't think today is a good day! Maybe I'll come back tomorrow."

This time when Daniel spoke to her, he waved the gun that was in his hand, as he gestured for her to come into the house. "Chrissey I'm not playing with your bi-polar, crazy, dysfunctional, psycho ass. Now would be the time for you to get your ass in this house before I step out onto the porch." Chrissey was shocked at the tone, but she would never show it.

Gaining boldness from the adjectives that dripped with disdain as Daniel used them to describe her mental capacity, Chrissey walked under the threshold. "And ain't nobody playing with your cheating, retarded, wining and dining, hotel spending, late night creeping, you wish your chick was dumb, having ass."

Without saying another word, Daniel, who stood a foot over Chrissey's frame, backed her into the living room with his eyes piercing into hers. And just when her breath caught in her throat, he turned from her and sat on the coffee colored sofa that Chrissey had skillfully hand-picked. He wondered to himself why he continued to deal with her dramatized actions when there were plenty of women who were willing to commit to him. He was a good-looking and well rounded individual. He reminded her of DMX and Chrissey was Gabrielle Union from the movie *Cradle to the Grave*. Lifting his head he asked, "Can you please tell me why you are so irrational?"

"What do you mean?" Chrissey asked somewhat confused as she joined him on the sofa.

"Why in the hell would you do that to my car Chrissey Rochelle Williams? What on God's green-earth possessed you to redecorate my damn car?" He yelled simply because he hated when she played stupid.

"What on God's green-earth would possess you to cheat on me?" She retorted.

"In order for me to cheat on you, it would deem that we are in a relationship, which you clarified was not the case!"

"So do you think that gives you walking papers to do whatever you want?" Chrissey questioned.

"Why not, you seem to!" He spat.

"Well then that's why your car looks like that! You've gots to be more careful!" Chrissey shrugged carelessly as she rested against the plush pillows.

Staring at her caramel complexion, Daniel couldn't help but love the way her skin glistened around the plushness of her lips. Rising to his feet, he sauntered over to Chrissey, grabbed a fistful of hair and harshly kissed her lips. When he pulled away, he watched her gasp for air as he walked to the front door, placed his hand on the knob and opened it. "Chrissey get out of my house before I beat you like a negro in the streets!" He ran his hand over his head and down his neck as he felt his body tensing. "My level of restraint is slowly slipping with you." He confessed.

Gathering her purse over her shoulder, she pranced towards the door. "Gladly!" When she crossed back over the threshold, she looked over her shoulder and stuck her tongue out at him! *I am such a stinker,* she thought to herself. "I've been thrown out of better places, Doc."

Behind the wheel of her car, Chrissey began thinking about that morning's events. She wasn't too worried about Daniel, he would calm down eventually. But, what had her life come to? She didn't want to commit to him because she wasn't alone, but somehow she'd become lonely. The only thrills that excited her were the unacceptable and hazardously insane dummy missions that she and her sisters created and conquered.

Before Chrissey knew it, blue and red lights reflected in her rear-view mirror and for a brief second, she contemplated out-driving the police in the S550 Mercedes Benz. All kinds of thoughts attacked her. *What if Daniel sent the police after her on a charge for Vandalism and Destruction of Property?* But then again, he wouldn't do that because it would draw too much attention to himself and his line of work.

Pulling over and putting the car in park, Chrissey rested her head against the headrest. She slowly rolled down her window to await the officer who was walking in her direction.

When the officer arrived at the driver door, Chrissey hadn't expected him to look so dreamy. He was tall and muscular, much too muscular for the uniform. His hazel complexion was a contrast to his chocolate eyes, but they twinkled with mystery and intrigued Chrissey. "Officer?"

"Ma'am do you know why I pulled you over?" The Officer responded.

"No Sir, I do not!" Chrissey smiled. She'd paid thousands of dollars to enhance her smile and she used it as a weapon whenever it deemed necessary.

"You were going ten miles over the speed-limit in a residential area. License and Registration, please." He recited.

"Actually, I don't have my license on me, but I can give you any information that you need."

"You don't have your Driver's License?" The Officer asked warily.

"No sir, I do not." She gazed up at him.

"Do you have an active Driver's License?" The Officer questioned. "Yes, if you want to run my information through the system, My name is Carla Camille Williams and I live on Independence in Southfield, Mi." Chrissey stated.

"Carla huh?" The officer eyed her suspiciously. "You know, normally when a driver rattles off their information like that; it usually belongs to a relative or sibling."

"Well, I'm sorry that you've had to entertain such foolery before now. But, if you would like to run my information then you'll find the truth."

"I'm sure I will, Carla. Give me your number!" The officer requested while pulling the pad out of his back pocket. He was trying to stay focused, but the head of his penis was twitching. He more so felt the seduction radiating off of her rather than seeing it. The longer he lingered, the more he felt the invisible thread drawing him closer to her.

Chrissey gave her real telephone number, but Carla's home information. The officer let her go with a warning and advised that he would be in touch. Chrissey needed a game plan and some finality in her life. Her new goal was to create an exit strategy from the tainted and deceitful environment that she had become prisoner to. Putting her car into drive, she pulled off from the curb and headed home.

CHAPTER 3

Hell hath no fury like a woman scorned!

Morgan was the only child and familiar with having no one to lean on. She was slowly drowning with the weight of taking care of her home: working forty plus hours a week, seeing after her six-year-old daughter and making sure that her man needed nor wanted for anything. With all the pressures of life, her castle was slowly beginning to crumble.

Morgan and her husband Brandon had been married for six years and although much time hadn't passed, it seemed as though they had changed immensely. Instead of enjoying each other's company, it seemed that lately, things had become more intense. According to Morgan's observation, Brandon's attention was diverted and her interactions with him had become few, far and in between.

In her mind, she felt that two could play this game and certainly she would win. Not because her husband wasn't a worthy opponent, but simply because she was more strategic in her approach-most women were. But before resulting to pettiness, she would do all that she could to save her marriage. Men were like machines and sometimes they needed to be oiled, but once they got going they would run like champions. Sex was normally that oil for their engine and Morgan had planned to give her husband all that he could stand.

Making a call to her best friend and her daughter's God-Mother, Morgan had asked Carla to keep Skylar for the night. Morgan had put a lot of thought into the events of the day. She had left work early and cleared her schedule for tomorrow because she was confident that she would need it. There was nothing more dangerous than a woman with a plan and a sex drive that didn't peak.

Pulling into the parking lot of Lawman & Associates, Morgan climbed her 5'9" frame out of her Infiniti truck and pranced towards the receptionist's desk. The name plate on her desk read Melissa, and the red headed, blue eyed lady greeted Morgan with an overly bright smile.

"Hello Melissa, I'd like to know if Brandon Morrison is available." Morgan smiled.

"Do you have an appointment?"

"No I don't, but if you let him know that Morgan Morrison is here, I'm sure it will be no problem!" Morgan offered a tight smile and quickly concluded that she needed to make more appearances in her husband's place of employment.

"Morgan as in his wife, Morgan?" The assistant stammered as she tried to confirm.

"Affirmative!" Morgan winked to take the sting out of her tone.

"Ohhhh, give me one second Ma'am!" Melissa quickly strolled towards the back and returned with Brandon close on her heels.

"Hey Baby!" He greeted and slowly pulled Morgan into his embrace.

"You got a few minutes for me?" She asked with her arms locked around his waist.

"I can always make time for you." Brandon grabbed Morgan's arm and led her to the furthest empty room within the rented space.

"Is there something wrong with your office?" She asked confused.

Taken back by her inquiry. "No, why would you say that?"

"Because you brought me into a conference room. If this is a bad time, I can just go!" Morgan was trying hard to calm her temper. There was already something about the secretary that she wasn't fond of and his behavior was adding to her suspicion.

Rubbing her shoulders and trying to dodge the fire in Morgan's eyes, Brandon explained, "I have a staff meeting in this room in about ten minutes. To avoid being late, I brought you in here to kill two birds with one stones."

Morgan ignored the cliché. "How long is the meeting?"

"An hour!"

There goes the surprise head that I was trying to give him! Morgan thought privately. "Well Babe, I see you're busy here, I'll just see you later."

"Wait, Morgan!" Brandon tried to grab her waist as she turned and walked towards the door, but she moved much faster than he expected.

When she got to the door, she opened it and turned back in her husband's direction. "It's cool Bae, I'll see you later."

Walking towards the reception area, she slipped the envelope over the counter and asked Melissa to deliver the small package to Brandon. Once she received confirmation that it would be taken care of, Morgan walked back towards the door. She had intentions of spending the rest of the day getting ready for her night.

Morgan watched the clock on the night stand as 7:00pm came and went without a single word from her husband. At 5pm, she had called the office to confirm that the envelope was delivered. Melissa gave her a litany of promises that she had personally hand delivered it to him. Morgan was trying to give her husband the benefit of the doubt when the phone rang.

Watching Brandon's face flash across the screen, Morgan answered it. "Babe where are you?" which is the calm version of what she really wanted to say. But age and wisdom had proven that it was easier to draw flies with honey rather than vinegar.

"I'm stuck in the office." His voice was muffled as if he was balancing the phone between his shoulder and his ear. "I don't think I'm going to make it!"

"You don't think you're going to make it?" Morgan asked in disbelief.

"I'm so sorry Babe, I was asked to close the deal on a Merger that's scheduled to take place by the end of the week." When he didn't hear his wife respond, he added, "I promise to make it up to you."

Morgan couldn't hold back the tears that stung her eyes. She could hear her husband calling her name through the headset, but she needed a few more seconds before bringing herself to answer. "I heard you, have a good night!" She whispered and then ended the call. Even if she decided to wait on him for a few more hours, the truth was that she knew her husband would be too tired to enjoy the rest of the evening. It seemed that the harder she tried, the more her efforts failed.

Morgan rose from the sofa with her phone still in hand as she snapped pictures of the bed that was covered in red and white heart shaped roses. Then she moved to the bathroom where additional rose petals covered the floor. The vanilla scented candles that lined the counters and shelves, had given the room the edge of romanticism that was needed while the chocolate covered strawberries promised pleasure, but all she received was disappointment.

Tears continued to fall as she walked into the area designated for dinner, the light from the camera flashed multiple times as she captured the champagne bottle, the three- course meal provided by room service and the handwritten love note. Not only had her husband wasted her time, but he had wasted her money as well. Morgan changed the setting on the camera, reversing it for an attempt on a "selfie". The first photo showed her flushed eyes and tear stained face, but the second selfie indulged her anger by capturing her middle finger. No one would have to speculate the message of the photo, it was a clear *fuck you*.

Morgan discarded her negligée as she put back on her clothes, quickly packed her suitcase and headed for the door. Once she reached the front desk, she asked for a printed receipt of all the charges for the services that were provided by the Renaissance Hotel and proceeded to check out for the night.

Arriving in Carla's driveway, Morgan's clock read 11:30pm; she figured that it would be better to call than to ring the doorbell at this hour. The last thing she wanted to do was scare Carla half to death.

"Hello?" Carla sleepily grumbled.

"I swear you are forever sleeping."

"That's what normal people do at this hour! What do you want? You're supposed to be screwing your husband's brains out for the second time tonight by now."

"I need to use your spare bedroom for the night. I'll get up and take Skylar to school in the morning."

Carla got quiet and whispered, "What happened?"

And before Morgan could censor it, she had burst into tears. She couldn't get the words passed her throat. There was no time to wipe the tears from her eyes and the snot from her nose when Carla began pulling on her passenger door handle.

When Carla slid into the passenger seat next to her best friend, she pulled her into an embrace. "Whatever it is, we can fix it. We're invincible. We're unbreakable. Whatever happened can be fixed." Carla recited over and over again until Morgan's body stopped trembling.

Morgan reached into the backseat of her luxury truck and handed Carla the photos that she printed at the nearest CVS when she left the Renaissance Hotel. Carla's mouth fell open when she shuffled through the pictures and she laughed when she saw the picture with Morgan and her middle finger. But, when she came across the receipts, a tear jerked in the corner of her eyes. "Oh honey!"

- Hotel Suite $469
- Dinner for Two $250
- Rose Petals $100
- Chocolate Covered Strawberry's $50
- Victoria's Secret $100
    o Lingerie
    o Candles
    o Fragrances

When Carla did the math, the total was dollars away from being a thousand dollars. She knew more than anything Morgan's feelings were hurt and that had hurt her too. "I'm really sorry Pooh!"

Morgan sniffled, "Don't be, because I intend to get every single penny back! Let's go in the house so that I can get some sleep." Morgan slipped in the bed, melting beside her daughter and slipped into a dreamless sleep. She'd found peace even when she felt there was none.

****

When Morgan arrived home the next morning, Brandon was sitting on the couch fully dressed. His eyes were red as if he hadn't gotten much sleep. When she stood in the doorway, his head lifted. "Morgan, where have you been?"

"Ohh, so now you care?" Morgan spat.

"Bae, I care about everything that revolves around you. How can you think I not care?"

"Hmm, well we could start with last night and then we can work our way through the last couple of months." Morgan folded her arms across her chest to restrain herself because he looked pitiful. Her first instinct was to comfort her man instead of disconnect from him.

Brandon had been prepared for the confrontation. He knew there were consequences for last night, so he mentally set his work aside so that he could emotionally be available for his wife.

"I'm sorry about last night, Bae." He apologized.

"Screw you!" She started for the stairs, but Brandon caught her arm. She tried her hardest never to cuss at her husband because he was a good man. Although, she would have paid big money for him to hear the vulgar language that was swimming through the sea of venom, that had pooled in her brain.

"Do you think that we live here for free?" He flipped the script since his sincerity wasn't working.

"What?" Morgan spun around at his query.

"I said, do you think that we live here for free? I provide for you and our daughter by busting my ass at work for you two." He pointed his finger at her for dramatic effects. "You have everything that you want because I make sacrifices - like last night - so that you can enjoy the life you live."

"I enjoy the life I live because I go to work everyday." Morgan countered.

"Excuse me? When you pay the monthly bills from the joint checking account, you must don't calculate that more than 70% of the money in that account is earned from Lawman & Associates. Every penny that I make is made available to you. I never ask for household contributions because *I AM YOUR MAN* and I enjoy seeing to your wants as well as your needs."

"And I try to see to yours as well, so what's your point?" Morgan stated calmly, although she felt anything but.

"My point is that disappointing you is never easy for me and I'm so sorry about last night, but I will not let us sink when there is so much money to be made. I'm a lawyer baby and right now I am swamped at work." He grabbed and wrapped his arm around Morgan even though she didn't hug him back.

"Tell me that you understand?" He breathed. "Tell me that you forgive me?" Brandon pleaded in her ear.

Morgan hated when he was sincere like this, it really lowered her defenses, but he wasn't going to win today. He might as well chalk that shit up. "Go to work Brandon, they need you!" Morgan pushed out of his embrace and headed up the stairs.

A little after lunch Morgan walked through the doors of Lawman & Associates, and of course she ran straight into Melissa. This time when she slid the envelope over the counter it was much thicker than the previous one. "Can you see to it that Brandon Morrison receives this package?"

"Sure thing!" Melissa sat the envelope to the side.

"Oh no, I'm sorry I should have been more clear!" Morgan smirked. "Can you give it to him right now?" She paused. "I'll wait!"

"But, he's in a meeting Mrs. Morrison." Melissa's eyes pleaded.

"Can you let him know that it's an emergency?" Morgan wanted to tell her that she didn't give any shits about his meeting; the whole damn building could burn to the ground as far as she was concerned.

With tight lips, Melissa nodded and backed her chair from the desk. Through the mirrored walls, Morgan could see the interaction. She watched the many faces that her husband made as he went through the photos and when he smirked she knew that he'd come across her personalized favorite (The middle finger). She even recognized the look of defeat when he looked at the bill from last night's arrangements and the sticky note on the top that read. "I WANT MY MONEY BACK!" Since his smart mouth ass contributed 70% of the funds to the joint account, then what's another thousand dollars to a boss?

Before Brandon could notice Morgan silently watching him, she exited through the door. She had been trying to keep calm, but the last couple of months had come full-circle. So today, she made a declaration *No more Mrs. Nice-Girl*, this meant war.

CHAPTER 4

Our Roots Say We're Sisters, Our Hearts Say We're Friends!

*C*arla was on her cell phone seated behind her desk talking to Joshua. During the week he stayed in Chicago to maintain his position and flow of income, but every Friday night he was in Michigan with her by 10pm. The space made her miss him more than she thought she could, but by the end of the week, space was a thing of the past.

Being almost seven months pregnant had interfered with a lot of events for Carla, but sex was not one of them. Her body lusted for him when he was away, but she craved him with an intense fire when he was near. She assumed that with time the passion would subside, but her kitty was hoping that it wouldn't.

When the figure walked passed her open blinds in her office, Carla recognized the individual immediately. "Babe, I'm going to call you right back." Carla didn't wait long for Joshua's consent before she hung up on him and sprinted towards the door.

Trying to catch up with his long legs, Carla called after him. "Brandon! Brandon!"

When he turned around Brandon smiled at the familiar face. "Hey CeCe, I didn't know you worked here!"

"Oh yeah, what are you doing here?"

He lowered his voice when he replied, "I've been assigned to head the merger between this corporation and Serenity Bank of Chicago."

Carla stood there with her mouth open. "Ya don't say!" was the only response that she could muster.

"Yeah. Your sister is still pretty mad at me about the other night, but I plan to make it up to her. Do you think you could keep Skylar if I give you the dates in advance? It will have to be after the merger though; I'm planning for a Friday thru Monday get away."

"I'd do anything for you guys." Carla smiled as her heart melted. She sincerely loved Brandon like a brother. "I just hope that you two plan on returning the favor in three to four months."

"Definitely. I hope that this getaway does the trick because if it doesn't then I'm doomed, big time."

"I'm sure it will, you know her better than anyone."

"No, I think you know her better than anyone." Brandon all but sighed.

"I know her personality, her actions and relentless attitude, but you have her heart. You know her emotionally… physically. You're her missing piece to any puzzle and her light to any dark path. You know what she needs."

Brandon looked defeated, so Carla came closer and hugged him, "Don't forget that. She chose you because you're her superman, but you have to be careful that you don't become immune to her kryptonite."

They released each other and Brandon looked as if a light had been shined on him, "I'll take care of it."

"Of course you will. You're a smart man!" Carla squeezed his arm.

Brandon kissed her cheek, rubbed her belly and moved in the direction of the exit.

Carla traveled back into her office with her mind swarming with questions! Brandon heading the merger reopened feelings that she had been trying to suppress. *Did Brandon have to interact with Dre at all? How much did he know about Dre's assets within the corporation?* She needed to get a handle on Dre before he resurfaced again. She knew that she needed to tell Joshua about her new lead, but it would have to wait two more days when she could see him face to face.

Sitting behind her desk, Carla sent an email to her sisters asking if they wanted to do dinner tonight at their favorite spot, 7pm sharp. Ten minutes later her computer chimed with four responses. A verdict had been made.

****

Seated with her back against the booth, Carla melted into her chair. The bigger she grew the harder it was for her to breathe, the harder it was for her to see and the harder it was becoming to hold her bladder. The slightest things made her pee on herself. Of course Joshua thought it was hilarious, until she accidently peed in the bed one night and it traveled to his side of the bed. That night, Carla was the only one laughing.

"Well, if it isn't the big girl!" Morgan greeted.

"Hi Pooh, how's my baby cooking?" Chrissey kissed her sister's cheek and rubbed her belly.

"Oh Bae, you're on time today?" Carla smiled at Chrissey.

"Um, don't be disrespectful!" Chrissey jokingly chastised.

"Where's Ebony!" Carla asked slightly concerned. "She's always on time!"

"She had a meeting at 5:30pm, she said she was going to be ten minutes late." Chrissey informed.

No more than five seconds later, Ebony entered the lively establishment. Joining her sisters at the familiar booth, she blew air kisses to everyone.

"Soooo, I'm assuming that you didn't get my email today?" Carla directed her question at Ebony before she could get comfortable in her seat.

Ebony looked a bit puzzled before realization dawned on her, "Oh, you mean the one from this morning?"

"Yes!"

"I got it, I just didn't read it!" Ebony confirmed as she slid her purse off of her shoulder.

"And why not?" Carla badgered.

Confessing, Ebony told her, "Because it was one thousand, three hundred and eighty-seven words Carla. I didn't have the time."

"Oh so now you're screening my emails through word count?" Carla was trying to simmer her temperament when Ebony didn't respond.

"Sister, I'll read it tomorrow!" Ebony cocked her head and forced a smile that she did not feel.

"Screw you and your tomorrow. I needed you to do it today!" Carla hated when her sisters were slowful in doing things that she requested. She often failed to understand that just because it was important to her, that didn't mean it was important to them.

"You do know that I am the oldest, correct? And you do know that you being pregnant doesn't make your issues my priority, correct?" Ebony chastised.

"And you do know that I have no problem coming across this table and beating your old ass, simply because I'm pregnant and you think I won't, correct?" Carla challenged.

"Time out - flag on the play, got dawg! What has gotten into you two?" Chrissey was a lot of things, but she didn't do a bunch of arguing and she didn't draw unnecessary attention to herself.

"Shut up Chrissey" Ebony and Carla chorused.

Morgan's burst of laughter prompted Carla to smile. "Brandon said he saw you earlier!" Morgan politely shifted the conversation.

"He did! And he also told me that you're still giving him the cold shoulder." Carla transformed swiftly, she'd deal with Ebony later.

Morgan laughed, "I am and I feel kind of bad because he transferred the money from the hotel expenses into my personal account several days ago."

"You got a good man, but I won't interfere with your training mechanisms." Carla respected Morgan as a friend and a sister, but she also understood the sanctity of marriage. If Carla's assistance wasn't sought then she didn't render it. "Chrissey what's going on with you and Daniel?" Carla shifted her attention to her baby sister.

"He's still mad too and he changed the locks on the condo door. I tried to go over there the other day, no luck." Chrissey shrugged, she wasn't pressed. It wasn't her style to be concerned, even if she cared. There were very few emotions that moved her, but caring wasn't one of them.

"Maybe you should try apologizing and actually meaning it!" Ebony suggested.

"And then she needs to be honest with him and herself regarding her feelings." Carla prompted.

"Holy Shit." Was all that everyone heard at the table as Morgan stared at the door. She tried whispering it, but failed miserably. It was almost as if she had seen a ghost.

Three pair of eyes joined Morgan's and suddenly everyone understood the reason that her mouth had slightly dropped. Before Ebony knew it their eyes were on her. As the figure slowly approached them, Ebony's heart rate continued to increase. If she had never saw him again, it wouldn't have been too soon.

As he approached the table, Ebony could smell his cologne. It was the same fragrance he had worn eleven years ago. The same smell that had brought her pleasure and pain. She had tried hard to exercise him out of her life, but the smallest things had reminded her of him and now he was here.

"Ladies" He greeted.

"Antoine." Everyone except Ebony responded in unison. She couldn't bring herself to say anything and she didn't trust her words to speak.

"Eb, You not speaking?" Antoine probed.

Instead of responding, she looked in her purse and retrieved a pen and began writing on the white napkin that her glass of water had previously sat on.

When Ebony slid the napkin across the table, Carla dropped her head in her hand and laughed.

Antoine leaned over the table to read it aloud, "No?"

Ebony wrote her response again, *NO*.

Antoine's frustration was slowly growing because she was embarrassing him. "Don't you think you're too old to play games?"

That was the second time someone had called her old within ten minutes. "No, I don't!" She finally spoke. "Do you think it was immature of you to leave me a letter after a two year relationship? Then have your corny ass stroll back in here eleven years later, like nothing happened."

"Eb, I'd like to talk!"

"And I'd like for you to die and go to hell, but we don't always get what we want, now do we?"

"Damn!" Chrissey whispered under her breath. She knew that Ebony could be just as mean as the rest of them, but they preferred her nice and loving.

Shaking his head at her candor. "I'mma see you around Eb, I know where to find you!" Without another word, Antoine had left as quickly as he had come.

Ebony blew out a long breath and Chrissey reached over and rubbed her back.

"Do you think that he knows?" Carla asked.

"Hell if I know!" Ebony whispered while trying to free herself from the memories.

At the same time that Ebony got up from the table to excuse herself, the food arrived. When she returned she continued the conversation as if nothing had happened. Ebony was the oldest and the most private of the three. Often times her sisters deemed her to be secretive, but she believed that she was just cautious. If something was wrong in her world, Chrissey and Carla had to pry it out of her. Unconsciously, she never wanted people to feel that she was a burden or that they had to fight her battles. She was the oldest and always acted as such, although, there had been a time or two when she needed her sister's rescuing.

"Okay, so tomorrow you turn seven months Carla, I'm thinking that we'll have your baby shower next month!" Ebony said as she reached over the table to grab a few chicken wings. If nothing else, Ebony was strategic and the topic of the shower was certain to do the trick.

Carla did the mental calculations. "Okay, so we'll have a June shower! Maybe we can turn it into a barbeque or something." Carla was starting to get excited. "Once we have a date, I can let Joshua know and he can make the necessary adjustments."

"You can use my house since my backyard is the biggest!" Morgan offered.

"How about your whole house is the biggest!" Chrissey bumped shoulders with Morgan. She couldn't hate and she wasn't going to lie, Morgan lived the life that most dreamed of.

"I'm just blessed!" Morgan replied humbly.

"And very well off!" Chrissey harassed.

"Well if you hadn't decorated my home so lavishly then no one would know!"

"Lies. All they have to do is turn into your Estates and they would know."

While everyone erupted in laughter, Ebony retreated to her own private thoughts. Regardless of what she thought and how she felt, she had to keep a smile on her face because her sisters were counting on her too.

CHAPTER 5

Avoidance Doesn't Equal Resolution

*E*bony tossed and turned most of the night. Whenever Ivan got up to use the bathroom or get a drink of water from the kitchen, she pretended to be sound asleep. The last thing she needed was her past coming back to make amends because as far as she knew, it no longer existed.

Ebony got up and proceeded as if everything was normal, just as she was programmed to do. She got Amber ready for school, cooked breakfast, prepared her materials for work and made Ivan's coffee. On her way out of the door, she kissed her daughter and turned to kiss her fiancé when he looked in her eyes and mouthed "Are you okay?"

Ebony nodded her head and kissed him long and hard, if she had said anything else it would have incriminated her. Sometimes it was hard always trying to be the strong one. Sometimes she needed for someone to hug and hold her just to say that it was going to be ok. Every once in a while, Ebony wanted to throw a pity party or have a temper tantrum, but the way her life was set up, there was no room for that.

Pulling into her assigned parking spot, Ebony opened the door to the back entrance of her event planning facility. Initially she had started out at home, but her clientele had grown so much that she opened up a shop in a strip mall off of the 696 freeway and 11 mile. She had hired a personal assistant (Jessica) and a store manager (Monica). Monica simply ran the office in Ebony's absence and she stood in the gap when Ebony needed to be in two places at once. Jessica had been a God-sent as she kept Ebony's books straight and her calendar, organized.

Not to boast or brag, but Ebony had done quite well for herself, and Ivan's background in Engineering was a definite plus. But if things didn't pan out for the two of them, then Ebony and her daughter Amber would still be able to maintain. *Eb's House of Décor* had continued to flourish more and more each year. After her third year of being established, she'd become a highly recommended service among businesses and venues alike.

It was 7:30am, Ebony had an event that she was planning for in the next seventy-two hours and she needed all the time she could get. The task of ordering tables, chairs, sashes, chair covers, linen, napkins and the materials for the center pieces that she needed to personally hand design had consumed more than an hour of her day. When the door bell rang, she pushed back from her desk and headed towards the front door.

"Hello Ma'am, are you Ebony Williams?"

"Indeed I am."

"Please sign here and I will go to the van and retrieve your package."

Ebony did as she was told and when the man returned with the most eloquent bouquet of flowers, her breath was caught in her throat. *These must be from Ivan*, she thought to herself. Whenever he sensed that she was in a bad mood, Ivan took whatever measure was necessary to alleviate the load.

Thanking the delivery man, she walked back towards her office as she searched for the note that should have been attached, but wasn't. The door bell rang again and the delivery man appeared.

"I'm sorry Ma'am; I forgot to give you the card."

Smiling politely Ebony took the card and her smile faded. The card read:

I told you that I'd know where to find you. I'd like to hear from you by noon, Today. I can be reached at: 248-965-5683. - Antoine

Ebony tossed the card in the trash and sat the flowers on the floor. She wasn't sure if she wanted to toss those in the garbage just yet, simply because they were beautiful. Antoine had a lot of nerve blowing in with the wind and then making demands. He had a lot to learn about the thirty year old Ebony because she had grown a lot since the age of nineteen.

Ebony shifted her attention back to her clients and the events that she had to cater for the week. She had caterers on hand that she utilized as well as personal gift shops and venues that she recycled. At 10am, Monica entered the office and performed her duties around the shop. Per the phone call from Jessica, there was a couple coming in to meet with Monica at 11am and then another one at 12pm.

Most people didn't know that Ebony was more than humble. She had picked Monica to be her face and meet with all potential clients before she agreed to take them on as clients. Not just because Monica was beautiful and built like a model, but she was also professional and discerning. Ebony's facility didn't do hood, they didn't do ghetto and they didn't do masses of drama. Ebony had made a vow that her professional life wouldn't be as chaotic and rambunctious as her personal life.

When Ebony finally lifted her head from her work, it was well after one o'clock in the afternoon. She pulled out the menu of her favorite delivery restaurant when Monica knocked on the door.

"Yes Ma'am, what can I do for you Mon?"

"Eb, you have a visitor!"

"Is it one of my sisters?" Ebony asked apprehensively.

"No, he said he's your husband!"

Confused and slightly irritated, Ebony walked towards the door when she saw Antoine approaching her.

"Honey, I've been waiting on your call!" Antoine walked passed Ebony and into her office.

Ebony rolled her eyes and directed her comment towards Monica, "Forgive this Jackass; he has the early onset of Dementia." She walked in the office behind him and closed the door.

When she approached him, he was staring at a picture of her with Amber and Ivan. "So this your little family, huh?"

With a tight smile, she replied, "It is!"

"So I guess there's no room for me?" Antoine inquired.

"No, there isn't!"

Antoine turned towards Ebony and grabbed her arm and instantly it burned. She hated when he touched her because just as always, a scorching desire surged through her and paralyzed her reflexes.

His hand traveled from her arm to her face as he cradled her cheeks and when he moved in to kiss her, her sex clenched. She wanted to stop him, she should have stopped him but she couldn't and well… she didn't.

He stroked his tongue inside her mouth, eliciting a moan from her. She felt like she was floating when her back landed against the door. He slid his hand underneath her skirt and stroked her sex with his fingers.

"Babe!" She moaned.

"I need you." He breathed into her mouth.

She heard him unbuckling his belt and unzipping his pants when she found her voice. "We can't!"

He didn't pay her any attention as his erection spilled out of his boxers as his pants puddled around his ankles.

Ebony's throat became dry as her body remembered the power of his stroke and resurrected the memory of his taste against her tongue.

Antoine registered the lust as he closed the distance between them with his erection resting in between her legs. "I got you, I promise." He mumbled.

His words vibrated throughout Ebony's brain and it sucked every piece of lust from her. She had heard that promise before and she knew that it was empty. She stepped out of Antoine's grasp, "Put your clothes on and leave my office."

"Eb, D---."

"Now!" If she heard one lie then she'd heard them all.

Just as soon as Antoine buckled his belt there was a knock on the door and before Ebony could say come in, the door opened and Ivan walked in.

"Babe!" Ebony addressed the man who stood more than a foot above her frame. He was silent by nature, but he walked with a presence that demanded respect and gleaned authority. He was six feet of pure luscious, honey skewed skin that was heavenly perfected to compliment hers.

Lifting his hand to stop her from speaking, Ivan questioned, "What's going on in here?"

"Nothing babe, he was just on his way out the door." Ebony tried to reason, but Ivan cut his eye at her.

"Aye guy, you got a name?"

"It's Toine."

"Is that short for something?" Ivan's irritation was just a notch below boiling.

"It's Antoine."

Ivan looked at Ebony and she silently shook her head. "*That* Antoine?" He asked her.

"Babe don't!" She pleaded. "Please don't!"

"You're asking me not to go there and y'all damn near in here fucking!" Ivan stated knowingly. He'd waited outside the door for the appropriate time to enter.

"Babe, I kissed him." She confessed. "I was wrong. Can we please discuss this at home?"

"Home?" He questioned. "You mean the same home where I pay all the bills? The home where I have been providing for you and his daughter that he left behind eleven years ago." Ivan yelled. "You mean that home, right?"

Antoine turned white as a ghost! "Whose daughter?" He looked at Ebony who had her hands covering her face only to look past her at the photo where the picture of the little girl was framed.

"Eb, you had my baby?" Antoine questioned. "Why didn't you tell me?" He took a step towards her.

When Ebony lifted her head, it was only to see Ivan walking out of her office and through the front door.

CHAPTER 6

What's Done In The Dark...

Chrissey walked into the bar and found a seat directly in front of the bartender. She wrapped her legs around the stool and rattled off her order of Hennessey and Sour. Unlike her sisters who had chosen careers in the office and behind desks, Chrissey was the free spirit. If she didn't love it, then she refused to do it. Her father sometimes acknowledged her as the rebel because she was the hardest one for him to raise. Maybe it was because she was the youngest or maybe it was simply because she reminded him of himself, just a female version.

"Every saint had a past and every sinner has a future," was one of her father's favorite quotes. He'd been a *bad boi* in his day, but Jesus redeems and saves. But, sometimes the sins of the father reside on the sons, but in this case, the daughters.

Sliding the glass closer to her, Chrissey gulped the drink. Wine was normally her drink of choice, but not after the kind of day she had. Her client fought her on every design that she laid out for her and after the three hour session, Chrissey had given up. Interior Design was not just her career, it was her life. It was instinctive and second nature for her, just as urinating standing up was for men. Well,

38

sometimes it was more on the floor than in the toilet, but we'll leave that discussion for another time.

Chrissey had lived in every loft, townhome, penthouse, apartment and condo that Downtown Detroit had to offer. Not because she couldn't maintain her rent, that was the least of her worries. She moved because she enjoyed decorating and filling the empty spaces. Chrissey enjoyed the look of astonishment on her guests' faces once they crossed over her threshold and entered into her royal queendom. Her home was breathtaking and it was a reflection of her complicated personality yet her sensual femininity.

Her clientele had been strictly word of mouth and then multiple referrals turned into contracts with establishments who were renovating and needed a keen eye to let the display speak for itself. Chrissey's inability to let go of men who dabbled in the streets wasn't solely monetary because she could hold her own. It was the rush and thrill of unarming and conquering someone who thought that their heart wasn't for the taking.

At first, Chrissey found it rather difficult to keep her attraction to the street world separate from her professional world. But, it didn't take much for her to learn that if she wasn't careful, she would jeopardize everything that she's worked so hard for.

As soon as Chrissey turned eighteen, one of her neighbors, who she named "FatButt" because of his beer belly, had made several attempts to grasp her attention. He would leave notes on her car, flowers at her parent's door and eventually he'd followed her when she left for school one morning. Of course she thought he was handsome, chocolate men with full lips were her weakness. And, she didn't mind the belly as long as it didn't interfere with the stroking. If his tits, stomach or thighs stuck out farther than his penis, then it was a no-go! FatButt had lavished her with gifts, shopping sprees and eventually bigger things like cars, jewelry and apartments.

For an eighteen year old, she was living the life. It was better than any dream that she could conjure up, until she realized how facetious fairytales were. Carlos, her father, had shielded her and her sisters from the dangers that waited outside of the four walls of their home. So when Chrissey had stepped outside of those perimeters, she was far from equipped.

Fat Butt played in the streets a lot; he would be in this club and that club. He would stop at this party or par-lay in a certain bar, but strip clubs were his ultimate pleasure. He loved beautiful women, whether they had clothes on or not and that's why Chrissey had become the ultimate target. Her soft caramel skin was accented with long wavy hair and a body that wouldn't quit. The only fat that was noticeable on her body was her ass and she completed several hundred squats a week to keep it that way.

One night, well into their two year relationship and after a laundry lists of disrespectful events that had previously occurred, Chrissey found Fat Butt in the strip club. She smiled at a few familiar faces and approached one of the bouncers who nodded towards the private room. He knew who she was looking for and he also knew how live Chrissey could get, so he complied and was cooperative whenever it deemed necessary.

When she walked into the room, there was one girl in between his legs and another riding his face. Before Chrissey could contain her rage, she gripped the first girl's neck and forced her face further down onto his penis until she began gagging and gasping for air. When the commotion disrupted the foreplay of the second stripper, who had taken his tongue on a merry-go round, Chrissey didn't hesitate. She swiftly hit her in the face, causing her to lose her balance. Although her rage was disastrous, her left hook was monstrous and FatButt was well aware. Visually locating the exit, he planned to slip out the room undetected, but Chrissey's adrenaline was just getting started. Aware of his size and height, she caught FatButt by the throat before he could slip off of the god awful looking sofa that smelled of sex and bodily fluids. The look of fear on his face as his wind pipe closed and the disruption of his breathing was unmistakably refreshing for Chrissey.

She didn't look back when he struggled for air and she could care less about the females who were sprawled on the floor. It took her forty-five minutes to clean out the apartment, leave the key on the table, get in her car and head back home. *Home* was a no judgment zone. One thing about her parents was that, no matter what you had done or who you had done, home would always be there.

Chrissey asked the bartender for a refill when a gentlemen motioned at the seat next to her. She'd frequented bars enough to know that he was asking if the seat was vacant. When he sat down and faced her, there was something vaguely familiar about him. He told the bartender, "I'll have what she's having."

"Do I know you?" Chrissey asked as he continued to stare at her.

"No, but I know you Carla!"

"Carla?" She winced; no one had ever mistaken the two. Although they had the same features their coloring was completely different. Chrissey was caramel, but Carla was a coco complexion and Ebony was a shade lighter than Carla. "My name is Chr ---." She stopped mid-sentence as the laughter sprang from her throat. "Ok, Mr. Officer." She raised her hands in a surrendering position. "You got me?" She giggled, the feeling from her drink had taken effect.

It wasn't the first time she had lied on Carla while getting a ticket and it probably wouldn't be her last.

"Chrissey, lying to the law is probably something you shouldn't make a habit out of!"

"Agreed." She took another swig of her drink. "So are you gonna arrest me or something?"

"I should because I know that you intend to drink and drive on top of the fact that you don't have a license."

Chrissey leaned closer and licked her lips, "Or... I could call my sister to come and drive my car home."

"Or..." He covered her hand. "I can follow you home and make sure you arrive safely."

Chrissey cocked her head to the side and squinted her eyes at him. No matter how hard she tried to give a man the benefit of the doubt, she realized that their asses were all the same. "Drive me home, huh?" She slurred her question, but he didn't miss the hint of sarcasm.

"You still live on Eastport, right? Apartment 316?" The officer asked.

Chrissey was confused and somewhat uncomfortable. "Is there something that I should know?"

"Yes, but I'll tell you once we leave." The officer rose from his chair and placed a ten dollar bill on the counter for his drink.

"Sure, we can leave right after you pay for my drink." She exclaimed.

"Pay for your drink?"

"Yes, I never entertain a man unless he has something to offer. Tonight, I'll go light on you and allow you to buy me a drink."

He hesitated before he pulled another ten dollars off of his money clip. "You're a piece of work." He said as he slid the money over the counter to the bartender.

"Indeed I am, but you're still short." She winked as she got up and made her way for the door. "I had two drinks." When he caught up to her, she asked, "What's your name?"

"FBI."

Chrissey waited for an elaboration, but it never came. He opened the door and motioned for her to walk thru it.

CHAPTER 7

You Can't Just Love Her, You Have To Show Her!

*M*organ walked into the private practice Friday morning with the weight of the world on her shoulders. She had a client in thirty minutes and she was trying to shake off the heaviness, but not even her caramel frappe' from McDonalds had been the cure. She felt like she was dying in her own marriage, suffocating from loneliness and bogged down with sadness.

Her husband had been so busy over the last week that he hadn't paid her any attention at all. He hadn't bothered to notice that she was still upset at him and that made her even more mad. When her intercom buzzed, Morgan knew that she'd have to hide her own sorrow to help others deal with theirs.

Morgan had been a behavioral therapist for the past four years and for the most part she had loved every moment of it. She helped people comprehend and sort through their issues and concerns and there was no greater feeling - it was her ultimate reward.

"Good Morning Destiny, how are you feeling today?" Morgan greeted her patient.

When Destiny smiled, yet remained silent, Morgan thought to repeat the question until Destiny opened her mouth to say, "I feel like I'm at the edge of a cliff and I'm about to fall off!"

Oh shit, well me too. Join the club. Let me get your retarded ass a parachute and hopefully your slow self will land on your damn feet. Morgan thought silently to herself, but instead she replied. "How so?"

After six clients with one hour designated for each client, Morgan was pooped. She didn't take weekend appointments because that was time set aside for her family. She cooked three meals a day on the weekends and she helped Skylar with any homework that was assigned and due by Monday. Whatever energy she had left, Morgan gave to her husband, which usually included her body and the rest she gave to Carla and her sisters which normally consisted of her mind.

The knock at her door came by surprise because her office assistant (Bridgette) normally used the intercom. "Come in!"

In walked eight men in a single file line with a dozen roses in an assortment of red, pink and white. Utterly confused and flabbergasted, Morgan searched for a card in every vase, but didn't find one. But she didn't need a card to tell her that her husband had sent them. This was his signature move when he wanted his wife to forgive him and normally it worked. For every time that he had to apologize he increased the vases by one more dozen and now he was up to eight.

Morgan pulled her cell phone out of her pocket to call him, but figured that she'd forgive him in person. Clearing her desk, she grabbed the light jacket that she carried to combat the mid-May weather. Reaching the front desk, she notified Bridgette that she was gone for the day and to take messages for any calls that she had.

When she stepped outside towards her car, it was missing and in its place was a black Lincoln Navigator.

"Mrs. Morrison?" The driver inquired.

"Yes!"

"I've been instructed to take you to your husband."

"And where is he?" She questioned.

"He's waiting on you ma'am!" The driver opened the door and Morgan slid onto the plush leather seats.

Morgan surveyed the spacious truck and rested her head against the seat as the driver began to pull out of the parking lot and towards the street. When the car stopped, she opened her eyes to find that she was in front of her home. Her husband was standing on the curb with two suitcases and the driver stepped out of the vehicle to assist him with putting the luggage in the trunk.

Morgan opened the door and Brandon slid in while she simultaneously straddled his lap. Lowering her face over his to greet him, she initiated a slow, passionate kiss that left her eyes shimmering.

While he tried to catch his breath, Morgan fumbled with the button and zipper on his pants. He tried to stop her with a silent reminder, "Babe, we're not alone in the car!"

"Then I suggest you be quiet, Babe!"

Morgan raised her hips as she slid her thong to the side and slid down the shaft of her husband's penis. She closed her eyes to stifle the moan that was bound to jump from her throat. It had been weeks since they'd been one and she knew that he agreed once his head fell back against the headrest.

Gyrating her hips and rocking on his hardening penis, caused Morgan to dig her nails into the leather of the seats. She leaned and whispered in his ear, how much she loved and missed him and in response he tightened his hold on her hips. Morgan wasn't offended that he didn't respond, she knew that he was communicating the best way he could without making a scene.

After Morgan pulled back, she tucked Brandon's penis back in his pants and cleaned the inside of her thighs before she whispered, "Where are we going?"

"Paradise!" Was the only response that Brandon rendered.

Morgan laid back against his chest and fell asleep. She didn't remember the five hour drive or when she'd closed her eyes. Once the driver announced that they had arrived, she moaned in response to moving off of her husband's lap. It felt like forever since the last time he had held her.

Stepping outside of the luxury vehicle, Morgan came face to face to what seemed like a palace- much larger than their estate.

She followed her husband's lead into the house and was greeted by a full staff. Brandon signed some paper work and they were shown to their room. When they arrived at their door, the name plate read: *PARADISE*.

Morgan smiled and squeezed his hand while he slid the key in the slot and opened the door. But, when she stepped into the room, it was completely different than what she imagined. There were mirrors everywhere- they lined the walls, ceiling and closets. There was a fireplace in front of the therapeutic king size bed, oval plush dining chairs with marble countertops and massage chairs. Although fascinated with the surroundings, it was the sixteen foot pool and hot tub that was on the other side of the sliding glass door, that caught Morgan's attention.

Turning in amazement to her husband, she asked, "Where are we?"

"Paradise, which is also known as Sybaris!"

"We're in Illinois!"

"Yes!"

"So does that mean you're going to take me to Chicago to shop as well?" Morgan smiled mischievously!

"If that's what you desire Baby, but it won't be today!"

Morgan walked towards her husband and wrapped her arms around his waist, "Babe!" She whispered, holding back the sappy emotions that she felt. "I absolutely love you."

Rubbing his hands over her cheeks, he brought his lips to hers. "Take off your clothes and meet me in the hot tub!"

Morgan stepped back and began to slowly undress, seductively smiling as she watched her husband watching her. He smiled, shook his head and turned towards the hot tub area.

She sat in between his legs with her head in the crook of his neck, "I could lay here with you, like this, forever!"

"I promised to make it up to you. That includes giving you my undivided attention for the rest of the weekend."

Morgan tightened her grip on his arms that were around her waist, "I miss you!"

"I know, Baby." He breathed deeply. "Some months I'm busier than others, but it doesn't mean that I've forgotten about you or that I love you any less." Brandon was silent until he heard Morgan sniffle. "I promise to work harder at trying to balance work and home."

Morgan sniffled again, "Sometimes I just wanna know that you love me. That you haven't forgotten about me, that I still own the key to your heart…" Morgan let out a big sob before continuing. "I know you're stressed and under a lot of pressure, but so am I, Bae. My job isn't easy either and after sitting and listening to people bitch about their problems all day, I just wanna come home to you. Sometimes, I just need to talk to you."

Brandon turned Morgan around to face him and she straddled his waist which was much easier when emerged in water. He kissed her tears before kissing her mouth. "Is that why you're seeing a therapist?"

Morgan sucked in a breath of air. "Who said I'm seeing a therapist?"

"I don't have to look at you everyday to pay attention to you! I am your husband. The first man you've ever loved, the first man to ever be inside of you." He whispered, "There isn't anything that you partake in that I don't notice."

Morgan settled her forehead against his, "Sometimes I feel like I'm drowning, Bae." She sobbed. "And sometimes I feel like I'm losing everything around me, where the only constant factor is Skylar."

"You're the love of my life, girl; you're the air that I breathe, Morgan." Brandon kissed her lips again. "When hell freezes over, you'll still have me." He moved to place her hand over his heart. "I love you with every fiber of my being, you are my entire world."

He lifted her out of the water and into the bedroom where he laid Morgan in the center of the bed. He spread her thighs as he covered her body with his. When he entered her, the sharp intake of air was the only thing to be heard in the room.

Morgan felt like she was sinking deeper with every stroke. He started out with long, slow, deep strokes to open her up. It has been at least a month since he'd been inside her-besides the car ride. "Daddy's sorry Baby," he whispered, "God, I'm sorry!"

Morgan's back arched the deeper he went, and Brandon gripped her hips to keep her from running. But, what he didn't know was that she wasn't running, she was trying to milk him for every stroke he had to offer.

"Please!" She cried when the first orgasm gripped her and her sex clenched. "Oh God, Bae, please!"

He pushed his hips further up, tilting his erection further towards her uterus and she felt her soul leave her body. She was floating as the first orgasm took her away. Brandon pulled out and slammed into her again and her sex clenched again as a second wave followed shortly behind it. The digging in his back told him that she couldn't take anymore, but he had planned to give his wife all that she could stand. In their entire relationship, he had never neglected her body. From this night forward, he was focusing on balance.

CHAPTER 8

Ain't No Fun, When The Rabbit Got The Gun!

While Brandon and Morgan were off doing God knows what, Carla was being harassed by a seven year old. Oh, the number of questions that she was asked and in turn, expected to be answered were beyond Carla's patience. Although Joshua had more experience with children, he seemed to make himself scarce, but Carla would fix that.

"Mama Cece?" Skylar walked in the bathroom.

"Yes Skylar."

"What time am I going to play with Amber?"

"What time is it, Sky?"

"It's 3:20pm."

"Well you have about thirty minutes before we leave the house."

"Is Joshua going with us?" Skylar asked.

"Yes, do you have a problem with Joshua?" Carla never thought to ask her before now.

"No, I was just asking." Waiting a few seconds, Skylar proceeded, "Mama CeCe?"

"Yes Sky."

"If you're my Godmother, does that make Joshua my Godfather?"

Carla paused. She hadn't really thought about it and she didn't feel comfortable answering on Joshua's behalf. "I think that's a question that you should ask him."

Carla watched Skylar walk out of the bathroom where she was pinning up her hair and into the other room where Joshua was. Stopping so that she could hear the conversation taking place, Carla waited patiently for Skylar's questioning to begin.

"Joshua?" Sky walked up to Joshua and stood beside him.

"What's up, Shorty?"

"If Mama CeCe is my Godmother, does that make you my Godfather?"

Joshua paused, counting the kids that he already had with another one on the way. He shrugged his shoulders, figuring that one more couldn't hurt. "Would you like for me to be your Godfather?"

"I mean since it seems that you're going to be around and with the baby on the way, I think you should claim me. I mean I'd hate for you to treat the new baby better than you treat me." Skylar cocked her head to the side as she stared up at him.

"How old are you again?" Joshua asked slightly taken back. He wasn't sure where the conversation would lead, but he wasn't expecting it to revolve around favoritism.

"I just turned seven. Hello, you have to keep up with these things if you're going to be my Goddaddy!"

"You're right Shorty, my bad." Joshua reached into his back pocket and pulled out a pen to take some notes. "When's your birthday?"

"January 15th." She stated proudly.

"And your favorite color?" Joshua continued to write as Skylar rattled off her favorite color, her favorite food, her favorite book and her favorite subject in school.

Meanwhile, Carla was in the bathroom laughing her tail off. *Joshua better be lucky we're having a boy because our daughter would be worse than Skylar.* Skylar would definitely give Joshua a run for his money if he wasn't careful. The running joke was that Skylar was more of Carla's daughter than Morgan's because they had the same behavioral traits. Carla believed it to be true because Skylar often made her head hurt with her overactive mind.

Thirty minutes later, Carla pulled up in front of Ebony's house to drop Skylar off so that she could play with Amber. Although Morgan and Brandon had left her in Carla's care, there was nothing for her to do at the house. Carla figured that Skylar would have more fun playing with someone around her age.

Scooting out of the car with her protuberant belly, Carla headed towards the stairs as Joshua got Skylar out of the car. Carla was almost positive that something had shifted between the two as Skylar clung to Joshua's hand. If Carla had any doubt before, she knew now that Joshua was going to be a wonderful father and she was looking forward to it.

Nearing the door, Carla noticed that the storm door was already opened and the screen door was unlocked. This was very unusual for Ebony because she was so anal about safety. Not knocking or waiting for someone to acknowledge her presence, Carla walked into the house only to stumble upon a scene that was slowly turning catastrophic.

Joshua came in behind her, but Carla raised a hand at him and shook her hand to stop him in his tracks.

"Pooh, what's going on here?" Carla called out to her sister.

"Go home Carla, today ain't the day!"

"Today ain't the day for what? To kill niccas?" Carla felt a sigh of relief as she heard the screen open and shut, which was confirmation that Joshua got the point. The last thing she needed was her Goddaughter to be scarred for life.

"Your sense of humor ain't working today Sweets, we should have did his ass in twelve years ago when he left me pregnant and then again the other day when he strolled his ass into Bar 7." Ebony was fuming.

"Ebony, you can't shoot him because you'll end up in jail and then he'll get custody of Amber. We wouldn't want an asshole like him to have that kind of opportunity, do we? I need you to put the gun down for sake of your daughter's livelihood."

"Not if I aim correctly. It will increase my chances of hitting the target dead on." Ebony repositioned the gun and she saw the pulse in Antoine's neck jump.

Antoine, who was never at a loss for words, didn't have many to say at this point. I mean what do you say to your baby mama when she has a glock pointed at your temple and she doesn't look like she plans on re-evaluating her game plan for today? Ebony wasn't budging, so Carla continued to negotiate.

"What about us, Ebony? What about Ivan? You're throwing away everything on a nobody!"

"This nobody just made Ivan pack all his things and leave me and Amber, so now we have nobody!" Ebony sobbed. "This douchebag is like a parasite, nothing good comes from being around him. Nothing good comes from allowing him into my space. He kills everything that he touches and he always leaves a trail behind as if to say, *I was here.*" Antoine had followed her home from her office, but Ebony was sure that after today, he'd never do that again.

"My daughter wasn't a bad thing, I gave you her!" Antoine said while still holding his hands in the air, but slightly offended by the poor description of character that Ebony had painted.

"Wrong answer, Jackass!" Ebony cocked her gun to the left this time. "That's my daughter, the only thing you contributed was your sperm, any dumbass could have done that!" She spat.

Carla dropped her head in the palm of her hands and shook her head. "Toine, how about you let me handle this." Carla came full circle and stood in front of Antoine, not to distract the gun, but to get Ebony to refocus on her. "We're better than this Bae, he's so not worth it. Ivan will come back. Do you know why?" When Ebony didn't respond, she continued, "Because he loves you! I know you're hurt, angry and pissed off, but we're gonna have to put this one in God's hands. Unfortunately, we're not gonna be able to kill him today, but I promise if he does anything else..." Carla shot Antoine a warning look, "I'll let you have at him."

With tears still rolling down her face, Ebony felt hopeful. "You promise?"

"Oh God, do I promise." Carla nodded and she stepped out of the way.

Releasing the clip, Ebony lowered her eyes. "Get out my house, Antoine, and for your safety, you better not ever come back. Next time, Carla won't be able to save yo raggedy ass."

"But, what about my daughter?" Antoine questioned.

"I'll see you in court if you wanna see *my* daughter and not a day before that!" Ebony put her gun down and picked up her Taser. Antoine jumped when the electricity vibrated through it. "Today!" She tapped the button on the Taser again. "I'mma need you to get your ass out my house, right now, today!"

Without another word Antoine left the house and Ebony silently prayed that it stayed that way.

****

Carla laid in bed with Joshua later that night, thinking that maybe she shouldn't have left Skylar there with her sister. Maybe she should have brought her goddaughter and her niece home with her.

"Don't do that." Joshua interrupted Carla's thoughts.

"Don't do what?"

"Don't sit there and stew with your thoughts, especially since I only see you three out of seven days a week." Joshua turned to Carla and pulled her into his embrace. "What's the matter?"

"I'm just thinking that maybe I should have brought the girls home with us!"

"Do you think that your sister is incapable of watching them?" Joshua calmly inquired.

"I just think that today was a lot for Eb and Skylar was only a few feet away in my car. It could have been much worse than it was!" Carla shifted in his arms. "I can hear Skylar now. *TeTe Ebony had a gun and a Taser and she wasn't afraid to use them. And Mama Cece told her that she could kill the man next time.*"

Joshua laughed at the picture that Carla mentally painted for him. "I think your sister has it under control, but calling to check on everyone couldn't hurt and it would help ease your mind." Joshua rubbed her stomach in a circular motion as the baby kicked back. Whenever he laid his hands on her stomach, his son never let him down- he always communicated back.

"You're right, I'mma call."

Twenty minutes later, Carla was back in the bed and Joshua was obviously still awake. When she slipped under the covers, in front of him, his erection welcomed her.

"Babe, you're thinking about sex at a time like this?"

"CeCe, I'm a man, I'm always thinking about sex." He lifted the hem of her night gown and ran his hand up and down the length of her body.

Despite how big Carla was getting, she tried not to deny Joshua sex because of how little time they spent together. But, if she had her way, she'd never have sex. Some people were blessed with high sex drives, while hers rarely shifted into gear. Now, don't get her wrong she was attracted to Joshua, but her hormones were all out of control. Although, all he had to do was touch her and she turned into a dripping faucet.

Joshua cupped his hand between her thighs and whispered in her ear, "Either you can get on top or I can stroke it from the back."

Without any hesitation, Carla climbed on top of him and caressed her clit with the head of his penis and within minutes, her kitty kat was a pouring waterfall.

CHAPTER 9

Strangers Can Be Angels, Unaware!

W hen Chrissey woke the next morning, her mind was filled with all kinds of scenarios that placed her at the center of the outcome. The asshole of an agent had given her seventy-two hours to make a decision. *What did he expect her to do?* Just turn over all the information that she knew without batting an eye? She wasn't set up like that, it wasn't in her DNA.

Getting out of bed, Chrissey glanced around her domain and deemed that all was well within her world, minus the added drama. She owned some of the most elegant and expensive pieces of furniture that were on the market and her walls were adorned with the most sophisticated portraits, painted by world renowned artists. Chrissey wasn't your average female; her interest went far beyond the materialistic possessions, lavish surroundings and imported goods.

She lived, breathed and moved in fashion, but she majored in Interior Design. She could make the simplest pieces correlate and she could turn a room from average to extraordinary. To say that Chrissey was talented was an understatement. Picasso splashed paint on walls, but Chrissey made the walls come alive and each one that she touched told a different story.

Glancing at the clock, Chrissey noticed that she had to meet with her sisters in an hour. Today, they would come up with a theme and shop for Carla's baby shower. Walking into the shower stall, she pushed all of her personal problems to the back of her mind, because there wasn't a thing that she could do about them at the moment.

Enroute to the store, Carla saw the reflection of a truck that was quite familiar in her rear-view. She was praying that it wasn't who she thought it was because she didn't have the strength to argue today. It had been weeks since they'd seen each other and it was partially because he hadn't called her. Chrissey wasn't the desperate type, caring was the last thing on her list of things to do and being vulnerable was never an option.

The phrase *Show No Love, Love Will Get You Killed*, always surfaced when she thought about giving a damn and then all feelings vanished.

It wasn't until the car pulled beside her passenger window and signaled for her to pull over that her suspicions were revealed. When she shook her head *NO*, the vehicle skated into her lane as if he was going to push her into on-coming traffic, leading to the opposite side of the street. Chrissey hit the accelerator and ran through the yellow light that would soon be turning red and the black Escalade truck continued in its pursuit.

Turning onto the service drive that led to I-75, Chrissey continued to pick up speed as she descended onto the freeway and in the direction of her sisters. Picking up her cell phone, Crissey dialed Carla's number all the while praying for traveling mercy and grace as the speedometer on her Benz pushed past 90mph. She knew that she was going to need some reinforcement since Daniel didn't seem to be in a playing mood today.

And Carla had just the weapon of choice that made a person think twice before proceeding. Their father had been completely against Carla's decision to get a gun because of her tamed, yet, unruly disposition.

Carla had only started carrying the gun when she couldn't decipher or anticipate Dre's, her ex-husband, next move. She'd told them that she would rather be safe than sorry! If Dre didn't give Carla some space then he was definitely going to be sorry. Carla's temper was certainly the foulest out of her sisters and it was simply because she was the nicest.

Wait, I know what you're thinking, let me explain. Nice people are relatively nice until they have to become nasty. And oftentimes they are meaner than those that aren't generally nice because they have to step out of themselves to address you. Carla turns into a Pitbull, mixed with a Rottweiler splashed with the hunt of a Lion and the prowess of a Tiger. If something needed to be dealt with, if someone needed to be dealt with, then she was always the last resort. Why? Because she showed no mercy.

Chrissy pulled into the parking lot of the store Party City and Carla and the others were already standing near their cars. When she put the car in park and got out, Daniel and those that accompanied him blocked her vehicle in and proceeded to do the same.

Daniel walked towards Chrissey with a heavy lethalness in his stride that made him more dangerous than she remembered. Once he got so close that his shadow blocked out the sunlight, Chrissey swung at him in defense, but Daniel grabbed her hand before the punch landed.

He leaned down so that only she was privy to what he had to say. "You better watch your back little girl, this is a big boy's game and I'd hate to see you caught up in the crossfire."

When Chrissey tried to shake her hands free, Carla cocked her gun to get Daniels's attention. Turning his head in her direction, Daniel said, "Ohhhh." He gave a wicked laugh. "Y'all some bad bitches today, huh? I guess you gon shoot me?"

Carla matched his laugh, "Without a second thought about it. I'll make sure to hide the pieces of your body in places that not even police dogs would be able to find them." Carla walked a little closer so that Daniel could feel her words. "So if you have a concern with Chrissey, or if there is a discrepancy that needs to be discussed, then that can be arranged. But, I assure you that the only funeral that we will partake in is yours," Carla looked at his entourage to extend the offer to them as well, "And anyone else that's connected to you. And if for one second you feel that I'm bluffing, then I encourage you to take a moment of silence and consult Jesus on the matter."

Without another moment of hesitation, Daniel let Chrissey go with a promise that he'd see her soon. As the parking lot cleared and the air begin to clear, Carla tried to shake off her agitation and Chrissey tried to calm her nerves while Ebony and Morgan watched in disbelief.

"What in the hell was that about?" Morgan asked. She knew that she should have talked Carla out of getting a gun. Carla wasn't stable enough to hold that kind of responsibility. *Who pulls a gun out in broad daylight?* Morgan thought to herself.

"I have no idea what his problem is, maybe he's still upset about his car." Chrissey answered, half lying, half telling the truth. She was almost positive that Daniel could feel the FBI hovering.

"Well, let's grab this baby shower stuff and get out of here. Chrissey, you can stay at my house tonight if you want!" Ebony offered.

"Ivan hasn't come back home yet?" Chrissey asked sympathetically.

"No." Ebony answered as she walked towards the entrance of the store. She hadn't been in the mood to discuss it and she still wasn't.

The Williams sisters strolled up and down each isle at Party City three times. They couldn't agree on a theme for the baby shower. While Carla was adamant on Turquois, Green and Yellow, Ebony insisted on challenging her on it. Morgan was bout tired of the foolishness altogether and Chrissey didn't care one way or another. It wasn't like she was the one having the baby, but she tried to shake the irritation because she wasn't even sure that was something she wanted for herself.

Did Chrissey really want to be like her sisters? Ebony had found a good man, but Antoine was her kryptonite. Carla had married a prince that turned into a frog and now there was Joshua who Chrissey was still trying to figure out. But, Morgan and Brandon were the average fairytale- boy meets girl, girl falls in love with boy, they have a child, they buy a big house and poof they live happily ever after.

In the midst of the chaos that the girls were creating in the middle of Party City, a woman who had been circling around them for the last ten minutes finally approached. "Are you all sisters?"

In unison the Williams' girls responded, "Yes!"

The pretty, yet strange woman who stood about five feet-five inches with short hair reminded them of Toni Braxton continued, "Are any of you married?"

Morgan responded, "I am."

Carla shrugged, "Divorced."

Ebony commented, "Engaged. Well at least I think I am!"

And Chrissey who never seemed to disappoint an awaiting audience responded, "Why? What can we do for you?"

The woman slightly ignored Chrissey and turned towards Carla to ask, "Since you're divorced, I wanted to know at what point do you call it quits in a marriage?"

Deciphering on a response, Carla could see the unshed tears in the woman's eyes and in the back of Carla's mind she thought *Lord, who am I to give counsel on the structure of marriage? Joshua's a Hoe, my ex husband is his pimp and I'm nothing more than another baby mama stuck in the midst of this shit.* But instead she replied, "Marriage is warfare within its own perimeters. It's a battlefield and whenever you feel that the fight has been placed on one participant's shoulders while the other seems unbothered, then you have to do some re-evaluating."

The stranger mumbled, "What if one spouse can't let go of the past?"

"Then you let go of them. You're human and we error. If God has forgiven us then we can't let others become an imprisonment for our indiscretions. If you've attempted to change and correct the error of your ways and that doesn't seem to be good enough, then you may have to gracefully leave the battlefield. Sometimes in order for true forgiveness to occur, separation must take place."

The lady moved closer and whispered, "I didn't know why I was drawn to you ladies and I didn't know how my intrusion would be interpreted, but you're the anointed one." She pointed in the center of Carla's chest. "I came towards sisters unaware of who or what I was searching for, but I was looking for you." She smiled at the others as she walked away.

Chrissey smacked her lips, "God doesn't just use you, we're all anointed!" She said as a matter of fact.

"Yes Bae, but Jesus is going to have to touch your nasty attitude... Miss. Why? What can we do for you?"

Morgan laughed. "She a lil devil, sent straight from hell, talking about she anointed though."

"Y'all have no chill." Ebony laughed.

Chrissey stood with her middle finger pointed in their direction. "F y'all man!"

"Are you going to church Sunday?" Carla sobered.

"I don't know yet!" Chrissey answered.

"You know mama is going to call you!" Carla reminded.

"What mama gonna do, whoop my behind? I'm a grown ass woman!" Chrissey challenged.

"I dare you to say it to her face, show her who's wearing the big draws." Carla joked.

Daddy wears the big draws." Ebony interjected.

"Watch it, daddy and I wear the same size." Carla chastised.

"Minus the hips!" Morgan added.

CHAPTER 10

It's My Prerogative!

Standing in the bathroom doorway, Joshua watched Carla in silence. The more her body expanded, the more beautiful he thought she was. Carla wore her pregnancy glow perfectly. There were parts of Joshua that didn't believe that he could love her anymore than he already did, but his emotions continued to prove him wrong. Carla had become his weakness and in this kind of game of love and war, *LOVE* was a weakness.

Sometimes he found himself being rough with her, but it was only because he was beginning to feel the weight of not being able to protect her closing in on him. Nonetheless, he would do it at all costs.

Carla's body was submerged completely under water with the only visible parts being her head and bulging round belly.

"What are you over there thinking about, Sug?" Carla had intruded in on Joshua's thoughts and she knew it, but, she hated when he stewed like that.

"I'm thinking about how close we are to the due date and we don't have a name for our son!" Joshua lied. It was easier than telling her that he was worried about the situation involving the half of million dollars and her ex husband. They were running out of time.

"Who doesn't have a name for their son?" Carla questioned, slightly lifting out of the water.

"We don't!"

"LIES!" Carla elevated her tone.

"What's his name then, Sug?" Joshua didn't feel like arguing with her, not today!

"His name is Joshua Reed Williams, Jr." She stated confidently.

"No, I'm not having it!"

"That's too bad because I don't recall asking you!"

"Isn't he my son too?" Joshua questioned.

"30/70. 30% you, 70% me."

"You're spoiling for a fight, aren't you?" Joshua asked.

"Of course I'm not, but you know that I am more than prepared to give you one." Carla smiled and sank back into her bath water. She closed her eyes, signaling the end of the discussion.

Joshua walked off annoyed. He figured that he should have just told her the truth instead of lying because it would have avoided any talk of the baby. Rambling into the bedroom, he heard Carla yell that her doctor's appointment was in an hour and for him to get ready.

During the last month, Joshua thought of all kinds of ways to tame Carla's mouth. But he realized that shoving his cock inside of her would only please her rising hormones, rather than control her. Maybe he needed to plan them a getaway, because he felt like he was suffocating.

Pulling into a parking spot at the doctor's office, they only saw four cars in sight. Very few gynecologists saw patients on Saturdays, but Carla had been fortunate to find one. She remained seated while Joshua came around to assist her. It wasn't so much that she enjoyed the chivalry, she just enjoyed his hands being on her body. Although he was seventeen years her senior- most women were repulsed by older men, but not her. He was very skilled in several areas that men within Carla's age bracket would have surely lacked in. After recently celebrating her twenty-ninth birthday, she was knocking on thirties door. Joshua had just celebrated his forty-sixth birthday and he was slowly but surely approaching the big five-zero.

Joshua left the signing in to Carla as he took a seat in the waiting area. Every time they entered the facility it gave him chills. He didn't care for doctors and he certainly hated dentists. But the power of a toothache could bring him to his knees at any place and any time. In his book, there was no comparison. He secretly wondered if that's how women viewed delivery. How far did it exceed past a toothache?

When Carla walked towards him, she noticed the change in Joshua's attitude. His normally relaxed posture was stiffer and his eyes had lost a bit of light from them. Sometimes he could be so closed off; sometimes she felt like his body was present, but his mind was a million miles away. Carla often wondered how she could fall in love with a man that could be hot and then be so cold. Which often led to her own concerns of how things would pan out, once the baby got here. Would Joshua soften up more or become more of a disciplinarian? For a man who had four children, she never saw any of them, except for that one night in her hotel room in Chicago last Fall.

Rising as their names were called and heading back to the exam room, Carla linked her hands with Joshua's. She needed the contact, she needed the reassurance that he was there with her.

While this was Carla's first child, this would be number five for Joshua. She didn't want to feel like this was just routine for him because this was special for her. This baby was special to her and the man himself was special to her.

Lying back on the exam table, Carla knew the things to expect:

- ✓ Cervix check (height, swelling, etc.)
- ✓ Urine tests
- ✓ Listening to the baby's heart beat.

Looking up from her chart the doctor addressed them, "It seems that everything is fine and progressing smoothly. The baby's heart beat is nice and strong. We'll schedule for you to do another ultrasound in one month. I know you mentioned that you wanted a 3-D photo and that can be arranged at that time. Are there any questions?"

Carla looked at Joshua and they both responded, "No ma'am."

Extending his hand, Joshua thanked the doctor and Carla proceeded to do the same.

Settled back inside the car with Joshua behind the wheel, Carla prompted conversation. "Babe, I just want us to be on the same page during and after the delivery."

"What are you talking about Carla? I plan to be right there. We discussed me taking a leave the week before the due date in case he comes early."

"Right, but I'm talking about my gift!"

"What gift?"

"My push gift!"

"Your what?"

"It's called a push gift. As in, I pushed your big head baby out of my small vagina and I deserve a gift."

"That's some ghetto shit you made up, didn't you?"

"No I didn't. Tamar asked for one."

"Tamar, who?"

"Braxton."

"Do I fucking look like Vince to you?" Joshua turned his head back to the road. He wasn't going to entertain her because she had officially lost her damn mind.

Sniggling, Carla silently assessed Joshua's slender, yet muscular frame. He reminded her of the actor Christian Keys, just not as light, with more defined, seasoned features. *What a man, what a man, what a mighty good man... Oh yes, he is.* The music had already begun to play in her head. "Just say that you'll think about it!"

Joshua knew that gifts were her thing. "What do you consider to be a push gift?"

"Certainly jewelry." She beamed.

"So you want a ring." Joshua established.

"I'd actually prefer it, if you want to give me a ring." Carla held out her hand and wiggled her fingers.

"An engagement ring?" Joshua asked.

"I'd take a promise ring. A nice, fat, expensive, several carat, promise ring."

Shaking his head, Joshua answered, "Okay."

Carla couldn't stand when he was dry like that. "Okay, what?"

"Nothing, I said okay. I know what you want, you asked me to think about it, I'm saying okay!" Joshua was officially overwhelmed.

Reaching over, Carla put her hands on top of his as they laid on the gear shift. "It's no pressure on the engagement ring. I know that's not something you've expressed wanting. But, I do love you and I'd like to spend my life with you as a family with our son."

"I know you do." Joshua felt a headache coming on.

"You know what?" Carla berated.

"I know that you love me and I know what you want!"

"So you don't love me?" Carla poked.

Joshua was counting in his head. On top of Carla being a bit of a psychotic individual, she was also hormonal. "You know that I do." Joshua's hand gripped the steering wheel a little tighter.

Carla shifted so that she could completely face him. "Then say it!"

"Say what?" Joshua knew what she wanted; he just wasn't in the mood for this shit today.

"Tell me you love me!" Carla demanded.

"No ---" Before Joshua could finish his sentence, Carla punched him in the arm, twice.

Recovering from the blow, Joshua calmly stated, "I don't have to tell you that I love you in order for you to know. Do I not show you that I love you?" When Carla remained silent, he pressured, "Huh? Do I not show you by driving from Chicago to Michigan every Friday night? Or making sure that I'm in attendance for every doctor's appointment? Do I not give you every piece of me when I make love to you? Have I not buried my secrets inside of you?" Joshua reprimanded.

"No you haven't." Carla pouted, "There are so many questions that I have. So many things that are unanswered about you. Like - who you are, where you've been and what you've been through!" The unshed tears had blinded her vision. She didn't know what had gotten into him, but she wouldn't bear the brunt of it because he was in a bad mood.

Carla hadn't realized that they were home until she heard him say, "Get out the car, I'll be back!"

Her first instinct was to ask where he was going, but her feelings were too hurt to even care. Joshua waited until she was in the house and the door was secured before he pulled off. There was too much weighing on him, too much coming for him at one time. He needed a release. He drove until he found himself sitting in one of the renovated warehouses that Dre had summoned him to on several occasions. The truth was that he hadn't spoken to Carla's ex husband since their deal went sour. Dre had hired him to seduce Carla and then turn her loose. Unfortunately he hadn't been able to hold up to his end of the bargain, because he'd fallen in love with her instead.

Joshua had been drawn to Carla even though it hadn't been his intent. The way she smiled. The way she laughed. Her untamable wit and quick sarcasm seemingly made him love her. There were several things that he couldn't stand about her that made him fall even harder for her - like her demanding attitude and unwavering stubbornness. She was relentless in her pursuit to get her way and she'd make you pay hell until you gave it to her. But, he often found himself still admiring her strength and the way that she loved her family, how she'd go to bat for them - right, wrong, or indifferent. Carla had a way about herself that made a simple encounter with her undoubtedly change a person, including him.

Popping the trunk of his Yukon, Joshua took out the contents and proceeded towards the entrance. When he approached the grounds, he gave the entry password **#entity** and was granted access. As he approached the front desk, he asked for Andre, but was quickly informed that he wasn't on the premises.

"If you'd be gracious enough to contact him, I'll wait for his return." Joshua was definite that once his name was given to Dre, he'd be sure to hurry in to see what he had to say. Forty-five minutes had passed before the service vehicle pulled into the parking lot and Andre, the businessman, moved towards the building. Joshua was sure that the business suit was just a front- he was a wolf in sheep's clothing realistically.

"Well, if it isn't the Iceman himself!" Andre extended his hand. Once Joshua shook it, he proceeded to follow him towards the back, for privacy purposes.

Behind closed doors, Andre unbuttoned his suit jacket and took a seat. "How's my ex- wife?"

"How's my daughter?" Joshua felt that one blow deserved another.

"You're still salty about me sleeping with your daughter, huh?" Dre asked, knowing the answer.

"You didn't just sleep with her, you also got her pregnant." Joshua corrected.

"Kind of like what you did with my wife at the time."

Joshua smirked at the reminder. "Solely with your permission."

Dre slowly nodded his head; he remembered in vivid detail the circumstances. "I heard that you two are having a son!"

"And I heard that my daughter miscarried your daughter!" Joshua was quick on his feet.

"Yeah, I'm still deciding if the shit was intentional or not." Andre confessed with a hint of resentment.

Joshua rubbed his hands together, "I've been doing some thinking and maybe it's you, maybe it's not the women!"

"Careful, you fucking son of a bitch." Andre warned without an ounce of tact.

With his hands in a surrendering stance, "Relax, that wasn't a shot, it was a suggestion. Maybe you should see someone about it, especially if children are something that you desire." Joshua was partially sympathetic on the subject.

Andre was a little uncomfortable with the subject and stood to his feet to level the playing field. "Maybe I'll do that!

So what the fuck do you want? I'm certain you're not here to discuss dick problems!"

"Certainly not. I'm here to discuss *our* problems." Joshua confirmed at the same time that the intercom came through announcing that additional visitors were requesting to join their meeting.

Cocking his head to the side with a sly smile, Andre stared Joshua in the eyes, "I'm assuming they're with you?"

"I'd never bring a knife to a gun fight." Was all the confirmation that Joshua rendered.

Pressing the button on the intercom system, Andre granted the secretary's request to see Joshua's guests in.

CHAPTER 11

If Loving You Is Wrong, I Don't Want To Be Right.

*E*bony tossed and turned for more than a week, she hadn't been productive at work and before long her business was going to suffer because of it. Which was the last thing that she wanted to happen, so she woke this morning with a new purpose. Rising out of bed, she went to the computer to search for the most recent transactions on the joint bank account. She needed to find her man, because the truth was that she wouldn't rest until she had.

What would she say once she'd found him, though? How could she possibly explain? The only thing she could do was pray that when she opened her mouth, God would help her find the words. She needed to mend whatever she had broken in their relationship. Ebony needed Ivan back.

The thought to simply show up at Ivan's job had crossed her mind, but it would only cause a scene and she didn't want to put his job in jeopardy! She just couldn't believe how she could be so stupid, allowing Antoine to come back into her life and within seconds cause havoc in her home. Ebony and Ivan had been friends for years, well before there was an Antoine to even think about. But, when Ivan went off to college in another state and left Ebony behind to take classes at a local college, Antoine had grasped her attention.

Just like every other girl she knew, Ebony had been dick crazy. Being a preacher's daughter hadn't meant much to her. As far as she was concerned she had her own life to live and she wanted to explore it to its fullest potential. But, once she found herself pregnant and at the mercy of her parent's forgiveness, she had to grow up and quickly. Ivan had come home during summer break, the semester before he was scheduled to graduate only to find the one woman that he loved more than his mother was barefoot and pregnant by someone else.

At thirty- one years old, Ebony had an eleven year old that only knew Ivan to be her father. Ivan had been there since the first contact at birth, but at some point she'd want to know the truth. At some point, Antoine would force her to expose the truth. And at some point, she'd have to.

Snapping the laptop shut, Ebony went in search of her clothes. If she made it to the hotel in enough time she could catch Ivan before he left for work. Per the transactions listed on the debit card, a charge to the Wyndham hotel's restaurant had posted, which was about ten minutes east of the house. In the back of her mind, she couldn't help wondering, if she really wanted him back. There was the one issue that had continued to nag her because it couldn't be overlooked. Grabbing her cell phone, Ebony called Carla to ask for some advice. When the connection broke, Ebony sighed thankfully that Carla had answered. Although, it was rare that anyone couldn't get in touch with Carla. It was a guaranteed fact that Carla always answered her phone, and that was why she was listed as everyone's emergency contact.

"Big sis, what's going on?" Carla answered her phone on the second ring.

"I need to talk, do you have a few minutes?" Ebony paced her living room floor.

"Sure, I'm on the other line with Morgan, but I can click her in too."

Before Ebony could protest, silence engulfed the line, signaling that she was too late.

"Okay and we're back." Carla enthused. She loved being the one to help her sisters, especially when she thought her situation was the worst.

"What's going on Ebony?" Morgan chimed. "How can we assist?"

Ebony was going to tell Morgan that she hadn't asked for her help at all actually, but she thought better of it, her professional advice would be imperative. "So you guys know that Ivan has been away from the house for over a week. We also know that he's a wonderful man and an even better father, but I'm wondering if I should go looking for him or just leave him be."

"But I thought you loved Ivan, sister?" Carla whined.

"I do, but..." Ebony's voice trailed off.

"But, what?" Morgan encouraged.

Ebony hated reminding people of things. "But, he can't have children."

"What do you mean he can't have kids?" Morgan probed.

"What does it sound like I said? We've talked about this, remember? When Carla was in Chicago." Ebony reflected.

"I remember, but it wasn't in depth. Have you ever been pregnant by him?" Carla asked.

"No!" Ebony was starting to think these two idiots were meant for each other. Were Carla and Morgan asking the same damn question, but rephrasing it each time they asked?

"Don't say it like that. I was thinking maybe you had miscarried and neglected to mention it or something." Carla scolded.

"What about seeing a specialist and having a semen analysis done?" Morgan offered.

"He won't go!" Ebony confessed.

"Well how do you know that there's really a problem?" Morgan asked.

"Because I went to the doctor and after some tests and blood work and a few exams, she said I'm fine." Ebony heard the whine in her voice a bit. The questions were starting to work on her patience and she was starting to regret asking for assistance. It was better that she handled it on her own, like she always did.

"So through process of elimination, you're concluding that it's him." Carla affirmed.

"Well this can be an awkward situation for any man, so let's try approaching this another way. Sometimes these things can be fixed by simple measures; sometimes it's not as bad as we believe it to be. There are these pills that a client of mine advised helped him and his wife conceive. It increases fertility in men." Morgan informed.

Skeptical, Ebony asked, "Are they over the counter?"

"Yea, you can get them from GNC." Morgan confirmed.

"It's not that horny goat weed, is it?" Ebony questioned.

"Horny Goat, what?" Carla interrupted.

"I've seen it a time or two when I went in to grab muscle milk at GNC. Next thing you know they'll have something that makes a man's nuts grow as long as a giraffe's." Ebony giggled.

"No, it's called fertility something, go in there and ask a representative." Morgan told her.

"Alright. I gotta go y'all, I'll call y'all back." Ebony hung up the phone before she let them say goodbye. They were overwhelming her by the second, whereas, she had bigger fish to fry.

She walked to the front desk of the four star hotel and advised that she had misplaced the key to her room. The receptionist asked for her last name and a new key was made without question or hesitation. "Will you need a late check out this morning?" The receptionist inquired.

"Can I let you know in about thirty minutes?" Ebony asked, while hoping for a positive outcome.

"Sure thing, have a wonderful morning." The receptionist smiled.

She was prayerful that it was going to be a wonderful morning, but in about three minutes, she would know for sure.

Approaching the door, Ebony had already begun talking to herself. She was reassuring herself that she could get her man back. Not only did she have the power of the pussy on her side, but she knew that she could conquer anything that she put her mind too. It was a motto that she had conjured with her sisters; *women ruled the world and men simply lived in it.*

Ebony couldn't decide if she should knock or if she should just stroll on in. She chose the latter. Sliding the key card in the door and watching the light go from red to green, her heart pounded. She turned the knob and proceeded to walk in when she heard the shower water running. She quickly concluded that this was an ample opportunity to seduce him. He was already naked, so she made her way to the bathroom as she undressed, leaving a trail of clothing as she went.

Gliding the curtain back she was glad to see that there wasn't another man in the shower with him. Of course that's a pretty shitty thing to think, but there were so many down low brothers in the world that sometimes it was simply hard to decipher. Seriously, he hadn't called in over a week and hadn't returned any of her calls either. A part of her feared that maybe she had finally given him what he needed to move on with his life. Unfortunately, women conjured up some of the most awful thoughts and escalated frivolous situations into severe ones – simply because it's in our nature.

As softly as she could, without trying to scare him, she said, "Hey babe!"

Turning towards the voice, Ivan's tense shoulders relaxed. He had felt her presence before he acknowledged her. He recognized her smell and scent before she opened her mouth. Ebony was his, she had always been his and nothing could change that. "Nice to see you cared enough to come find me." He sarcastically replied. Ivan knew it was only a matter of time before Ebony found him. Ebony and her sisters were like a pack of wolves that could find anything and locate anyone.

Before Ebony could climb in the shower with him, he replied, "I'll be out in a minute and we can talk then."

She tried not to show her embarrassment. She was standing there booty-butt ass naked and he expected her to just go and get dressed? Yeah, that's not how this game was supposed to go. "I'd rather talk in here." She said.

"I'd rather not." He countered. When he saw the hurt expression in her eyes, he added, "I don't want to be distracted, I want to talk. So get dressed, I'll be out in a minute." Ivan turned his back towards her to signal finalization.

Ivan was always even tempered, but he had a rough side just like everyone else. Ebony had thoroughly tested that side.

Stepping out of the shower, Ivan mentally went over the demands that he expected from Ebony. He had a long week to think everything through and he was ready to discuss his terms. As an intentional distraction, Ivan walked out of the bathroom with his towel wrapped around his waist. And as expected, Ebony glanced over his body- starting with his neckline and then over his collar bone.

She tried to make her eyes glance faster, but the longing and appreciation that she felt towards his body was hard to disguise. The way his muscular chest separated with precise definition made her mouth seem to water a bit. Antoine was a prowess in the bedroom, but Ivan was strategic, his ultimate goal was her satisfaction. He was thorough and tender and she absolutely loved him. She had always loved him. He was her knight in shining armor and somehow she always seemed to be the damsel in distress.

To avoid looking into his eyes, Ebony clasped her hands together and squeezed them in between her thighs. Ivan recognized the sexual energy. He may not have been her first, but he certainly knew her body and he recognized the signs. She was like a vampire in need of blood, yet, he watched her fidget in silence.

"So you want to talk?" He asked breaking the silence while embracing the tension.

Finally looking up at him, Ebony felt foolish. He wasn't going to let it go that easily. She was going to have to beg. "Yes, it's been over a week. I figured that I'd give you some time to calm down, ya know?" She slumped her shoulders. "Possibly forgive me!"

"What is it that you need to be forgiven for?" Ivan crossed his arms over his chest to help her focus on the conversation and not his manliness.

Ebony's eyes dropped again, he was going to make her confess her sins before forgiving her. "I'm sorry for making you question my trust and loyalty to you by kissing Antoine. I was completely out of line and I promise that it will never happen again."

"Are you sure that he's not what you desire?"

"Of course not!" Her eyes pleaded. "That's why I'm here!"

"Is that why you're here?" He questioned. "I thought you were here because you never go longer than a week without dick." He insulted.

"You know what?" Ebony rose from the chair. "Fuck you!" Grabbing her purse, she walked towards the door, but before she could grab the handle, Ivan grabbed her upper arms.

Turning her around and pressing her body against the door, Ivan melted into her. When he tipped her chin to look in her eyes, he saw how misty they were. "Why you crying?"

"Why would you talk to me like that?" She shoved him, but he didn't budge. "There's nobody I love more than you, you have my heart and you know that." The more she sniffed, the more tears fell.

"I don't feel like you love me." He whispered. "You around here kissing niccas, letting them feel on you- giving away privileges that they haven't earned. You embarrassed me as a man, as your man." He explained calmly.

"I'm sorry." She paused to wipe her nose. "I don't know how many times you want me to say it. I messed up and I need you to forgive me. I'll do whatever it takes. I'll never find another man to love me as you have. I'll never find a man who will love Amber the way that you do – to teach her how to love as you have. No one could replace you - they wouldn't do your role justice." She paused again as she cupped his face in between her hands. "The position is unfillable."

"And you want to make it up to me?" He asked.

"Yes," Ebony whined. "Whatever you want me to do!" She reiterated.

"Then marry me."

Sobering quickly, "Huh?" She glanced at her left hand where the diamond engagement ring was housed. "I thought we were already engaged to be married?"

"I'm tired of the procrastination. I think I've been patient in this pursuit and this engagement has run its course." He grabbed Ebony's face to make sure that she stared directly into his eyes. "Marry me."

"When?" She whispered.

"Today!"

"Today?" Ebony panicked.

"Yes!" Ivan replied. "Be my wife, give your daughter my name. Make us an official family." He hadn't taken his hands from around her arms, giving her a gentle squeeze. "No more games."

"But, what about our families? I want my daddy to walk me down the aisle; your mother to give her blessing. Our friends? Bridesmaids? Groomsmen?" She rambled.

"Right now, at this moment, I don't care about any of that. I don't care if they're included or not. This is about you and I." Ivan caressed her cheeks. "How we feel in this moment and what we feel in our hearts."

"But, we don't have a minister, the rings, a marriage license nor a witness." Ebony tried to reason with him. She knew that he could be irrational when he set his mind to something.

Ivan finally released her and walked towards his suitcase where he pulled a copy of a marriage license and two velvet boxes out. "I've got two out of four, but there's a chapel downstairs. And if you want your family here, then I'll give you two hours to do what you need to do before meeting me in the chapel."

Ebony stared at him as if he'd seriously gone crazy. "I need at least four hours and I have to pull Amber out of school. I want her here for this."

Ivan mulled it over, it was 11am now- four hours would be enough time. "Okay, I'll give you four hours; meet me in the chapel at 3pm."

Ebony rubbed her hand up and down his chest and finally rested them at the knot of the towel. She closed the space between them and gently rubbed the imprint of his penis. "3pm, don't be late."

Ebony tightened the hold on her purse and ran out the door. Her first call was to her parents and then her sisters, informing them to meet her at the chapel at 2:30pm. She knew how this worked and you never gave guests accurate times because they always showed up later.

Ebony was a planner, this was her profession. She had always envisioned her wedding day looking a certain way and she intended to get as close to it as possible. Finding the nearest David's Bridal, Ebony gave herself thirty minutes to get in and get out. She walked towards the prettiest dress in the shop, almost as if a magnet had drawn her to it. When she checked the price tag it was only nine hundred dollars. Amber was going to be her flower girl. Stumbling upon a white beaded dress with an olive green ribbon, confirmed that this was the dress. Instinctively, she texted Ivan with the ribbon attached and instructed that he wear a tux with a vest and bow tie that matched the color scheme.

After waiting on hold for fifteen minutes, Ebony was able to reach the chapel at the hotel. Securing the photographer and videographer that they offered at such a late hour has costs her five hundred dollars for two hours. She wanted to negotiate the terms because she was born with a gift of persuasion, but time wouldn't permit. Her event photographer that she kept on hand had taken the week off and retreated to the mountains with his pregnant wife. Ebony had no choice but to suck it up and bite the bullet. She refused to let money be the reason why the most important day of her life wouldn't be photographed and filmed. Ebony vowed to do this one time and one time only.

At 12:30pm sharp, Ebony walked into her cousin's salon for the impromptu appointment. She looked at her and said, "I need an up-do with lots of curls."

The stylist hesitated, "Am I allowed to attend? I mean I know that it's a small, private wedding, but…"

Ebony tapped her arm, stopping her mid sentence. "Of course you can, as long as you get there by 3pm." Pulling out her cell phone. "Matter of fact, I'm going to make a post on Facebook and all that can get there, can come." She laughed out loud as she typed, unsure of why she hadn't thought of that an hour ago. Knowing Ivan, Ebony was sure that he hadn't told everyone so she sent a mass text to her family and friends and then another to Ivan's family.

By 2:30pm, Ebony was back at the hotel and fully dressed. Amber excitedly waited in the corner with her basket and flowers while Carla was tying the back of Ebony's dress. Carla was just about to pull the veil over her face just as their dad, Carlos walked in. His eyes watered a bit, "Well I certainly believe that it's about time, how's my baby girl doing?"

"I'm nervous daddy, but I'm on cloud nine, how's Ivan?"

"I've never seen him so ready. He's a fine man and he'll make an even better husband." Carlos kissed her forehead.

"That's a lot coming from you daddy."

"I know." Carlos laughed.

Ebony and her sisters fought and argued about a lot of things, but the one thing they agreed upon was the counsel of their father. They had always been able to take his word to the bank. If he didn't like a boy or man that they dated, then they discarded them. But, because the Williams sisters were emotionally challenged, it took them some time to loosen their attachment to the particular guy, but eventually they did.

"Alright, let's not keep the groom waiting." Chrissey added. She had just tied the ribbon on Amber's hair.

"Did you tell Morgan?" Carla asked Ebony.

Nodding, Ebony explained, "Her secretary said that she was booked for the remainder of the day, but she'd give her the message and Brandon was in court."

"Alright well, let's get going, there's always pictures." Carla walked towards the door to take a seat next to her mother. "Oh mommy, she's beautiful." Carla whispered.

Eileen decided to wait before seeing the bride. Special events like this made her overly emotional, so she trusted her daughters to take care of their sister.

As Ebony walked down the aisle, Carla ran her hand over her belly. She couldn't help imagining Joshua standing at the altar. She wanted this; she wanted the chance of a real family- a happily ever after.

The exchange of vows and sealing it with a kiss made Carla's eyes misty. She couldn't tell if it was because of her raging and illogical hormones or if her happiness was just that uncontainable. Nonetheless, Carla had gained a brother that was more than worthy of her sister.

Chrissey walked over to Carla, "Sis can definitely bring a crowd together at such a late notice, can't she?"

"Yeah, I didn't expect to see so many people. The chapel was full." Carla agreed.

"And how in the hell did she get a wedding cake at this late hour?"

"She is an event planner Chriss, I'm sure she pulled some strings." Switching the subject as smoothly as she could, hoping that Chrissey would take the bait. "Are you keeping Amber tonight?"

"What? Repetí Por Favor." Chrissey replied.

Carla smacked her lips, "Oh now you speak Spanish?"

"No hablo, no inglés." Chrissey turned and walked off after the statement.

Carla grabbed a handful of rice and threw it at Chrissey because she got on her damn nerves. Carla was pregnant and not in the mood, but Chrissey was never in the mood. Long ago, Carla reasoned with the fact that Chrissey was just naturally an asshole. But, she's never understood why men loved the shit out of her. Meaning, she couldn't rid herself of them. Men would call her, stalk her, buy her expensive things and treat her like a goddess, meanwhile Carla only saw her as an asshole that had a rare tendency to be nice. "What a dick!" She murmured out loud and went in search of the dessert table.

****

Ivan upgraded the room to a Honeymoon Suite. The room was double the size of the previous one. The hot tub was in the middle of the floor with rose petals that traveled from the center of the bed to the rim of the tub. He had carried his bride over the threshold and he planned to thoroughly execute his rights as a husband. It had been one week too long.

"Baby, can you help me?" Ebony asked as she presented her back to him.

"It would be my pleasure." He obliged, combing his hands over her shoulders and down her back. She shuddered under his touch as he brought his mouth to the side of her neck. "I love you." He moved to the other side of her neck. "And I love your body."

Ebony laughed, "I love you more."

"Show me." He whispered.

Stepping out of the wedding gown, Ebony turned and began to undress him. The lovemaking was slow and intimate. Ivan stroked a little longer and Ebony dug her nails a little deeper. She felt as if she was floating on top of her body. Ivan had never loved her the way that he had in that moment. Something clicked. Something had bound them together- a three fold cord that's not easily broken. And that's bible.

CHAPTER 12

Many Are Called, Few Are Chosen!

*C*hrissey needed a sisters meeting and she needed a sisters meeting now. Sending a message on GroupMe to her sisters, she arranged for everyone to meet at Bar7, by 6pm. It was the middle of the week and everyone had their own lives to attend to, but some things couldn't afford to wait until the weekend. She tried to handle her affairs on her own because she felt she had to prove that she wasn't just the youngest of the Williams sisters, but she was the most independent. Although, some things were simply out of her control.

When her sisters all sat down, Chrissey said, "You guys might wanna grab a drink for this," As she signaled for the waitress. Each sister completed their order and stared silently at Chrissey. She pulled her cell phone out of her pocket and requested for them to listen as the voicemail played:

> *Chrissey, I sincerely love your ass, but if you think for one second*
> *That I'm going to let you play me for some sucka ass nicca*
> *Then you've got another thing coming sweetheart. After everything I've*

Done for you, after everything your psycho
ass has put me through
There's no way you're getting off the hook
that easily. Running your mouth
To people who can't protect you from me, is
a major mistake. What I loved
Most about you was your street smarts, but
maybe I was wrong because
That was definitely a dummy move.

Carla was annoyed. "Is he seriously still mad about what happened last week? How old is Daniel?" Carla wanted to call him something other than Daniel, but God had been dealing with her about her mouth, so she chose the latter.

Chrissey shook her head. "He's forty-four."

"Damn, is he really that old?" Morgan asked.

Ebony whistled. "That's a nice looking old man."

"With his bald headed a-, behind, with his baldheaded behind." Carla commented and corrected herself.

Chrissey cocked her head. "Are you giving up cursing?"

"Ummm, something like that!" Carla partially confirmed. She didn't need her sisters ragging on her, so she shrugged her shoulders as if it wasn't a big deal.

"Ohh, I can't wait to see this shit." Ebony added.

Morgan was always stuck in the middle when the air got a little thick between the sisters, even though she was just as curious to see this transformation like the rest of them. Carla had been cussing as long as Morgan could remember. "Okay Chriss, so what are you gonna do about Daniel? What do you want us to do?" Morgan felt a little bit of bile rise up in her throat and she was doing all that she could to settle her stomach.

Chrissey sighed, she hadn't really thought much about a plan, but she did feel better letting them know what was going on. Or at least part of what was going on. "I just needed to talk; do you think you guys could come over for a little while?"

Calculating the amount of gas that she used just to talk, Ebony questioned, "So why the hell did we come here, you could have told us this at your house. Now we gotta drive all the way from Southfield to Downtown?"

Hating the fact that her sister was such a cheap ass, Chrissey retorted, "No one ever thinks about me when I have to drive from Downtown to Southfield to see y'all!"

"Then maybe you should move a little closer. Don't get mad at us because we live near each other." Carla reprimanded.

Requesting the check and leaving a tip behind as they exited the restaurant, Chrissey began to look around her. She had become so paranoid over the last week or so. It always felt as if someone was watching her every move. Daniel thought she made a dummy move, well that made him an even bigger dummy for leaving a damn voicemail. What kind of street nicca does that? A dumb one, she concluded.

She entered her garage and waited for her sisters to walk from the visitor's parking spots assigned by the Condo Association. Smirking as she listened to her sister's groan and complain about the long walk to her front door. Chrissey couldn't help thinking *Oh the joy of having sisters.*

With all the murmuring from her siblings as they entered the house, Chrissey ignored the fact that the light at the front door entrance didn't come on so she moved to the nearest lamp to obtain some light. Screaming and jabbing at the figure that was sitting on her twelve hundred dollar sofa was all that Chrissey could do to avoid being piss poor scared. "What the hell is wrong with you? Why would you just sit in the dark like that? How did you even get in here?" She interrogated.

Ebony, Carla and Morgan stood still in confusion as they watched the scene play out before them. Obviously Chrissey didn't need their help, but when the rather large gentlemen flipped her on her back and covered his body over hers, they concluded that she was no match for him.

"I didn't mean to scare you, well at least not to the degree where you begin to pounce on a federal agent."

The sisters looked at each other as he identified his position and the rank that he had over the situation.

Chrissey threw her hands in the air. "Aww well fucking sue me. This is trespassing as well as breaking and entering."

"God, that mouth of yours could use some soap." The agent snarled.

"Don't worry about my mouth; you need to worry about my left hook." Chrissey challenged.

"I could just arrest you."

"Arrest me for what?" Chrissey yelled as her eye grew large.

The agent cocked his head and stared at Chrissey long enough to catch the hints of beauty in her eyes, but short enough for her not to notice. He slowly rolled off of her and helped her to her feet. "Obstructing my investigation."

"That's bullshit and you know it!" Chrissey went to shove him again, but thought better of it.

"I don't know anything because you haven't told me anything!" This time he was firm in his delivery.

Carla whose bladder was slowly letting her down made her way to the bathroom while Ebony and Morgan made themselves at home on the sofa. Chrissey rarely ever let anyone sit in her front room, but they deemed today to be special circumstances. There's no way they drove thirty miles to sit in the other room and pretend to be nosey when they could enjoy the front row seats and make their observations with certainty.

Chrissey exhaled and tried to calmly explain her position, "There is nothing to tell you. I don't have the information that you think I do. I don't have the relationship with him that a normal girlfriend would have!"

"Then tell me what you have!" The FBI agent challenged.

"What's your name?" She snapped her fingers like she was searching for his name in her memory bank. "Mr...?"

"You can call me James."

"Okay James," Chrissey continued, "I fuck Daniel's brains out. I drive him wild and he gives me money. I drive his cars and every now and then I roll over and play dead when I don't want to be bothered. And if I'm feeling real kinky..." She walked over to James and got real close and lowered her eyelids to give him a taste of seduction and said, "Then I get me a side nicca who holds me over until I'm willing to deal with Daniel again." She pushed his chest and yelled, but noted that his packs were hard as bricks and the shove was harmless to his frame. "Now do you get it? He's nothing more than a jump off that I happen to care about. There's nothing more and nothing less to it."

"Oh, but there is more, who is Angela?" He questioned.

Chrissey paused briefly to weigh her options, but quickly decided that she had nothing to lose. "It's his damn wife and he has a daughter named Tasha, who might be able to give you some information as well, but I can assure you that my chunky cheeks can't help you. Now will you please step off before you get my ass killed?" Chrissey turned around to address her sisters because she neglected to mention some relevant information to them, "Umm close your mouth bitches before some flies land in it, I'll explain later."

"Later my ass." Ebony mumbled.

"Do you think he'd hurt you?" James questioned.

"Hmm let me see, do I think he'd hurt me? Do you think I'd say it if I didn't?" Chrissey moved her hand to grab ahold of James concealed, yet muscular biceps. God, there was something spectacular and sexual about a man with shoulders that made her purr. "Why? Are you gonna protect me Mr. Government?"

"I certainly intend too!" It had been some time since James had spent time with a woman because of his personal preferences to maintain his career. But, he was never too involved with a job to comprehend when a woman was flirting with him.

The tension and rousing of emotions continued between Chrissey and James so long that Carla, Ebony and Morgan decided to leave them to it. Who could protect her better than the nice piece of specimen who had graced her home. By the end of the heated discussion, James decided he had burned enough energy spinning his wheels with such a feisty, hard-headed, complicated, yet intriguing woman. If he weren't careful, he would be sure to find himself spinning in her web.

The weekend had come and gone, but not before Chrissey's phone rang right before ten a.m. with Carla yelling on the other end of it. Chrissey swore that Carla's pregnancy was making her much crazier than normal or it could have been Chrissey's refusal to attend Sunday morning service this morning. But, it wasn't until Carla started crying and blubbering about how Chrissey was always making things difficult and everything wasn't always about her and how she felt, that she caved. It really annoyed Chrissey how selfish her sisters believed her to be. She simply beat to the rhythm of her own drum and because she didn't have a man or children, she didn't owe anyone, anything!

Pulling back the covers of her Egyptian styled bedspread, Chrissey moved briskly through the house trying to make a cup of coffee- which she rarely drank. Except for instances such as being bullied into doing things that she didn't want to do- like going to church this morning. While the coffee brewed, she stepped into her custom walk-in closest and moved toward the white color coded section. She was feeling kind of sanctified this morning and what other color could display such an aura for an angel- other than white.

Forty-five minutes later, Chrissey sat outside of the beautiful brick building that she had personally over-seen in the conception of the exterior and interior designs. The pulpit had been personalized to fit her father's personality and favorite colors of royal blue accented with gold trimmings. The bathrooms held ceramic tiles and some of the most elegant portraits that conveyed the beliefs of Faith, God and Family. She believed in all three and she agreed with the mission statement of the church, but it was her own convictions that kept her away. Most preachers' kids had a gift or a talent, some of them were just as anointed as their parents and eventually accept their fate.

But preachers' kids like Chrissey, ran. It was so much easier than submitting to what God wanted her to do and being who she was called to be. She wasn't ready to give up her lifestyle. She wasn't ready to change the way she talked because got dammit, she enjoyed. She didn't intentionally try to make people jealous of her, but she understood that they were and she certainly didn't mind giving them something to be jealous about. But if she surrendered to God, then what? What would come next? After another ten minutes of pep talk, Chrissey got out of her car and moved towards the entrance. She hated when the ushers acted as if it had been that long since they had saw her. Their excessive hugs and the extra ten seconds that they took to rub her back, was annoying. Chrissey knew she was a heathen, she didn't need these assholes to remind her. She was just about to change her mind and walk back out the door when the man to her left caught her eye.

"Holy Shit." She swore under her breath and then quickly said sorry to God for cussing in his house. James nodded in her direction and then scooted over a chair to offer her the end seat.

When she took the chair that he offered, he said, "Looks like you were gonna run!"

"Yep, straight to hell if I don't get it together!" She replied. "What are you doing here?"

"Covering all my bases!" He commented and turned his attention back towards the front where Carla and Ebony were beginning to take the stage. Carla was the first one to speak:

> *"Praise the Lord everybody, come on and clap your hands.*
> *Come on and bless him. I know some people believe that their alarm clock*
> *Woke them up this morning, but how many know that it was Grace and Mercy*
> *That renewed? How many know that it was in divine order that God allowed your*
> *Eyes to open, for your hands to clap, for your feet to stomp, for your mouth to open and*
> *Your tongue to work? Well then you might as well come on and bless him. For his*

> *Goodness and his mercy. Bless him, simply because he's worthy, because he's God and God alone. Because he is Alpha and Omega, the beginning and the end, because he holds All power. Oh Glory, won't you help me bless him?"*

Chrissey stood back in admiration. She had always been secretly jealous of how Carla could go into the presence of God, how she could summon God's attention and how he would simply respond. Chrissey had become so caught up in her observation that she didn't hear Carla beckoning her to join them on stage in praise and worship. An usher appeared near her seat and politely helped her stand to her feet and make her way to the podium. As she retrieved the cordless mic, Ebony led them into a familiar song of worship. Chrissey was so enthralled in the spirit that she began to lead the song and her sisters backed her up. One song led into another and before anyone knew, deliverance had come. From the looks, you couldn't tell who had done more weeping- the praise and worship team or the congregation.

As Pastor Carlos Williams took his place at the pulpit, he began his sermon of forgiveness:

> *"Today's sermon starts in Matthew 6:14-15 NIV*

> **For if you forgive men when they sin against you, your heavenly Father will also forgive you. But if you do not forgive men their sins, your Father will not forgive your sins.**

> *Also in Ephesians 4: 31-32 NIV*

Get rid of all bitterness, rage and anger, brawling and slander, along with every form of malice. Be kind and compassionate to one another, forgiving each other, just as in Christ God forgave you.

I hear some of you and you're thinking, okay Lord, I've forgiven them already, yet they have constantly abused the fact that I have turned the other cheek. What more shall I do? If you look over in Matthew 18: 21-22 NIV, the bible reads:

Then Peter came to Jesus and asked, "Lord, how many times shall I forgive my brother when he sins against me? Up to seven times?" Jesus answered, "I tell you, not seven times, but seventy-seven times."

Then there are those individuals that are much stubborn than Peter and you're not willing to take the risk in forgiving nor are you willing to make a fool of yourself in that particular situation and you're at the brink of throwing in the towel, remember John 8:7 NIV refers to the woman who was caught in the act of adultery:

When they kept on questioning him, he straightened up and said to them, "If any one of you is without sin, let him be the first to throw a stone at her."

Now that we understand that we have to forgive others in order to be forgiven, let's take the time and forgive ourselves. Sometimes we take the hard road and we continuously beat ourselves up for the choices and the decisions that we've made. We've committed adultery, we've fornicated, we've had children out of wedlock, we've disappointed our families, we've let ourselves down and we've hooked and manipulated those who trusted us. Some of us are masters of deception and we're wondering why God just won't throw us away already. I want you to know that it's simply because his grace is sufficient and his love is limitless. You're worth fighting for and his blood washes white as snow.

Sometimes we think we're the black sheep of the family, when really its our own condemnation, our friends and family have forgiven us yet we're still beating ourselves up. Nobody can whoop yo butt like you can. Half of you are running from God, running from the call on your life because you feel that the things that you've done and the things that you've suffered deems you unworthy. Some of us have betrayed God, abandoned our call and shunned our anointing simply because his will isn't what we want to do. But how many know that God is married to the backslider? God already knows that we're gonna mess up - that our best is as filthy rags. You have been bought with a price and this life is not yours to live. Turn to your neighbor and say:

God has already forgiven me, now I have to forgive myself.

The worst kind of bondage is bondage of the mind. Once your mind has been compromised, then the devil can control the rest of you. Turn to another neighbor and say:

I plead the blood of Jesus over my mind. I know who I am and I know whose I am.

Hug your neighbor and say God Bless You!

****

Church left the Williams girls feeling some kind of way. Chrissy was obviously convicted because it was something that she had struggled with daily. Her mother had always called her a prophetess, told her to watch what came out of her mouth because her words were powerful. She looked over at James and wondered what he was thinking because of his closed expression. She wondered if he had his own skeletons deeply hidden. A government profession such as his didn't leave much for a social life.

Carla had sat next to Joshua during the service and although he had remained quiet, every now and then he'd give her hand a bit of a squeeze. It was their secret code when they agreed that something was relevant in the message. Carla didn't know a lot about Joshua's past, but she knew that he had some secrets, some that he wasn't quite proud of. Carla herself had shame that she dealt with more than unforgiveness. Her current situation didn't leave her in the holiest position. She didn't care much about what people thought, but surely she cared that she had offended God. She never wanted her behavior to delay her blessings. That's why she had been working on her mouth and the things that came out of it. Some things were out of her control, like being pregnant, but the things she could control she would begin to do so. As long as God could spare her a little more grace in the fornication department until after she had the baby, then she'd eliminate that too.

Ebony hoped that Ivan had fully listened to the preached word. It was so on time. That's why she loved God so much. Simply because he was always *ON TIME*. She had made a mistake, one that slightly haunted her. Even though Ivan had forgiven her, she knew that he'd never forget. It would be so much easier to walk away and start over in a new relationship, but God had confirmed over and over again that this relationship had been ordained by him. So she'd take the time, fall back, enjoy marriage, forgive and be forgiven and allow God to be that, God.

There was an unspoken agreement that their mother, Eileen always made Sunday dinner. Even when Chrissey missed church, she never missed Sunday dinner. Immediately following service, everyone pulled up to the three story, four bedroom, two car garage home in Farmington Hills, Mi, where the Williams' had resided for decades. Carla was the first one out of the car, food was all that she could think about.

As she entered the front door she yelled, "Mommy, I'm home. What did you cook?"

"Scoot over Big Bertha!" Chrissey gently shoved Carla and Ebony snickered.

"How about you two set the table!" Eileen suggested.

"Mommy, I was going to help you in the kitchen." Chrissey whined.

Carla smacked her lips; Chrissey was always trying to get out of manual labor. "Why? Were you gonna do the dishes or something? Mommy doesn't need your help; she needs you to set the table because my feet are swollen." Carla wiggled her toes that slipped out of her shoes the moment she hit the door.

"Well if you keep your feet down on the ground and not up in the air, then maybe your feet or any other part of your body wouldn't be swollen." Chrissey insulted.

"You know what home-wrecker…" Carla's voice trailed off when Chrissey walked towards her. "What you gonna do pimp? You ain't really about that life!"

"Won't y'all two take a time out?" Ebony suggested.

"Nobody asked you little Miss. Goody –Two- Shoes." Chrissey responded.

This time it was Carla's turn to chuckle. "She swears she's the boss of us."

Chrissey turned towards Eileen. "Mommy, she also thinks that she's your favorite."

Carla chimed in. "And that she's the only one who looks like you! I mean we all know that Chrissey's adopted, but I'm definitely your daughter." Chrissey was the lightest of her sisters and it had always been a private joke amongst them.

"Alright, Alright, Alright, that's enough!" Carlos had heard enough. Nothing made his head hurt more than having all three of his daughter's under the same roof. It brought back the horrible memory of him being in a house with teenage daughters and a premenopausal wife. Oh the travesty of being the only testosterone in the four walls.

"Daddy, tell Carla to apologize!" Chrissey urged.

"For what?" Carla yelled.

"For the insult!" Chrissey stated.

"Before or after you called me Big Bertha." Carla squealed.

Carlos started taking off his belt; the clinging of the buckle caught their attention.

"Um Daddy, I'm pregnant, you can't whoop pregnant people." Carla was the first one to try her luck. "Chrissey on the other hand could use a whooping. I don't think you chastised her enough growing up."

"What the hell? I got the most whoopings!" Chrissey recalled.

"Because you were bad and nothing much has changed in that regard." Carla confirmed.

Their men simply looked on. Ivan was used to it and Joshua was slowly becoming accustomed, but James was appalled. Surely, Chrissey wasn't the same woman who had flirted with him, gotten smart with him and had attempted to hit him. This was going to be an enjoyable evening, he thought to himself.

Carlos finally spoke to end the rivalry between the two sisters. "Carla set the table and Chrissey you have dish duty."

Carla grabbed the table cloth and stuck her tongue out at Chrissey, who met her with the middle finger. "Ohhh, I'm telling Daddy."

"You bet not or I'll give you the most hideous baby shower of your life." Chrissey threatened.

"Satan." Carla called and walked passed her.

Chrissey slapped her hand to her chest, slightly appalled by the remark. "I'm an angel."

"Yeah, an angel of death." Carla called out.

"Chrissey bring that young man in here so that I can officially meet him." Carlos yelled from across the room. "You know that nobody is a stranger at my table so I'd like to know him so that he doesn't become one."

James rose from the sofa and extended his hand, "Sir, my name is James Pierce and I enjoyed your Sermon today, I believe that it was certainly spirit led."

"I believe in the leading of the Holy Ghost. Where you from son? Where do you work?"

"I'm initially from Tampa, Florida and I work for the United States Government." James answered as truthfully as possible.

"A working man, that's exactly what you need Chrissey. Somebody to settle down with that has real pay and benefits."

"Um, Daddy. It's not like that between us." Chrissey discouraged.

"Oh, but it will be." Carlos confirmed and turned his attention back to James. "I swear she gives me the most grief. It must be because I dropped her as a baby." Carlos sniggled and returned his focus to the television.

"Daddy you did not drop me that was Carla!" Chrissey corrected.

"No, Carla rolled down the stairs, Ebony rolled off the porch and you slipped out my arms. I'm your daddy girl, I know." His smile was unforgiving.

"Mommy!" Chrissey yelled.

Eileen had no words for the foolishness that her daughters started, but her husband stirred. She raised her hand and shook her head signaling that she wasn't having it. "That's between you and your father."

Chrissey looked at James and she turned her back to hide the emotions lingering in her features. Without further conversation, he returned back to his seat. Carla felt bad for her sister. Chrissey was embarrassed because she never brought boys home and the one time that she does, Daddy embarrasses her.

"Daddy, don't forget that the baby shower is in two weeks." Carla swiftly changed the subject. Her sister rode her nerves to no end, but she was still her sister. She'd protect her against all odds even if it was against their father.

Carlos mumbled some form of compliance under his breath. It was a known fact that he thought baby showers were events that men had no place in. The only time he made an exception was for one of his daughters.

With the table spread, everyone sat down for Sunday brunch and the conversation continued as Chrissey continued to stir mischief. "This house sure does hold some memories." Turning towards her sister, "Carla do you remember that time daddy took your phone for sexting that guy you were so infatuated with?"

"Which Guy?" Ebony chimed in. "You know Carla crushed on a lot of guys."

"Ma?" Carla looked at her mother for some help and then to her father. "Dad?" When neither parent said anything in her defense, she pretended to roll up her sleeves. It was time to get down to business. "I do remember. But do you remember when Daddy beat your butt, for sneaking that guy in the house Chrissey? He tore all the skin off that pink tail of yours, didn't he?" Carla laughed.

"Not as bad as he beat Ebony for that guy she snuck in!" Chrissey shot.

"That's because he stole all daddy's jewelry." Carla laughed some more. Shit, Chrissey had gone back in time at least seventeen years. It was funnier to Carla because she was smart enough to leave it just at sex-texting. Monkey See, Monkey Do didn't apply to Carla because she learned better from observation, there was no need to repeat her sisters actions.

Ebony was annoyed rather than amused. "At least mommy and daddy didn't have to tag team me for fighting each other outside the school with a whole audience watching."

This time Eileen and Carlos both laughed. They remembered the scene vividly. Eileen had pulled up to the elementary school and Chrissey and Carla were throwing blows. They were only in the third and fourth grade, but it was the first and the last physical fight that they had outside of the house.

Little did the children know, it broke Eileen's heart to whoop them because she left the disciplining to Carlos. Nonetheless, she meant it when she told them that they fought together, they didn't fight each other. There was another incident a year or two later, when Eileen came home to find Chrissey sitting on the porch because she jumped out of the bathroom window to escape Carla's wrath. It had taken a few years for Eileen to catch on to the fact that Chrissey usually initiated the fights, but Carla was hell bent on resolving them.

Carla cut her eyes at Joshua who had been in tears since the first verbal punch was thrown. "I told Mommy that Chrissey hit me first. She was showing out just like she always has, acting like she's the boss of me." Carla stabbed her fork into her plate harder that necessary. "Bald headed butt, get on my nerves."

"Oh, but you love me though." Chrissey flicked some mashed potatoes across the room at Carla. "Gon head and scoop it up, I know you wanna eat it." Chrissey teased. "Fat butt."

"At least I got a butt." Carla charged.

"What are you talking about? I got a butt."

"How much did it cost you?" Carla questioned. She knew it would add to the embarrassment that James was simply taking in.

"You dirty little…" Before she could finish her sentence she felt her father's eyes on her. "You know good and well that I haven't paid for any parts of my body."

"I don't know anything, prove it!" Carla stuck her tongue out.

Chrissey picked up her knife this time and Carla smirked with the reply, "Checkmate!"

"You gon walk forward, but you gon limp back." Chrissey recited.

"Well come on then Cletus, come on." Carla laughed.

Dinner concluded with more jokes and stories. Of course Eileen and Carlos could have stopped their daughters at anytime, but no one could embarrass them more than they could embarrass each other. After the dishes were cleaned, each daughter and their companion took a spot. Ebony and Ivan took the back porch. They had called Morgan to check on Amber, who had been spending time with Skylar. Chrissey and James took a walk around the property, while Carla and Joshua copped a seat on the front porch.

"You know your dad just tolerates me, right?" Joshua asked Carla when she swung her legs across his lap.

"Has he done anything that makes you uncomfortable?" Carla asked, concerned.

"Naw, but I'm a daddy, I know."

"Everything's gonna be ok once the baby gets here." She whispered. "This baby is destined for greatness, born to bridge together every gap." She grabbed Joshua's hand and placed it on her rounding belly, locking it in place. "His presence alone will correct every wrong for your family and mine."

"And how do you know this?"

"I've been talking to Jesus about JJ, watch what I tell you!" Carla stated as a matter of fact.

"Who in the hell is JJ?" Joshua asked with much irritation.

"Uh hello, Joshua Jr." Carla knew that her father had an issue with Joshua - Joshua's age and Carla's pregnancy, but if nothing else, Carlos was sensitive to the leading of the Holy Ghost. And just as God had revealed the destiny of Carla's unborn child to her, he'd do the same for her father, for peace sake.

Joshua went to protest, but thought better of it. He wouldn't ruin the perfect Sunday that they were having. But he'd have to tell her why he didn't want a junior and soon. He didn't need anyone carrying on his name or legacy. "Whatever!" Joshua turned his attention back to massaging her feet that seemed a little more swollen than usual.

CHAPTER 13

Be Careful What You Ask For!

*J*oshua had taken off a half day of work. By noon, he was sitting behind the wheel of his car driving from Chicago to Michigan. By 5pm, he estimated to be sitting outside of Serenity Bank waiting for Carla to walk through the doors. According to his calculations, they should arrive in Pittsburgh, Pennsylvania by 9:30pm.

Walking into the Grand Hotel, Carla was awestruck by the ancient palace styled interior. The king size bed was only accessible by climbing the four steps and walking onto the platform that it was housed upon. Decorations of lush pillows and sheer curtains hung from each angle of the bed, securing the privacy of lovers.

The hot tub was positioned in the center of the floor, small enough not to manipulate the space of the room, but large enough for both of them to fit comfortably. The subtle seduction of romanticism was suggested in each area of the room and Carla welcomed the ambiance. She bumped shoulders with Joshua and he shook his head with a smile and proceeded to put away their luggage. No words were needed, he registered the shimmer of excitement in her eyes.

He was aware that Carla's first order of business would be to eat and then he'd coax her to take a bath with him. He just needed some alone time with her in a space that he was familiar with. Pennsylvania was his home and he wanted to share it with her. Tossing the menu on the bed, he instructed Carla to make some suggestions. "You don't mind if we stay in today do you? I'd like to show you some things, tomorrow."

Glancing over the menu, Carla replied absentmindedly, "Whatever you want babe. I don't have to eat now, we can order something a little later, I have a bunch of snacks in the bag."

"All that sugar and salt is why your feet are swollen like that." He chastised, but Carla remained silent. She no longer desired to argue with him when he went into daddy mode. There was no need to remind him that she wasn't a child, she preferred showing him.

Without another thought, Joshua began filling the large tub with water until it passed the jets, setting the timer to sixty minutes. Kneeling in front of Carla, he began removing her shoes, then unbuttoning her pants. After sliding them down her legs, he lifted her shirt over her head and leaned over and whispered, "I need you naked."

Carla loved looking at Joshua especially when he was catering to her; he was pretty for a man. He had smooth skin with fine hair that showed his mixed ancestry and she hoped that those features passed on to their son. She didn't know why she loved him so much, but she did. He had given her a child, his seed, and he'd been there in ways she never expected. He had a weird way of showing that he loved her, but she was learning to respect it.

Looking at the hot tub filling with water for the first time, she asked, "You want me to ride?" She knew that the closer she got to delivery, the more she had to avoid the hot water, but this was just one night.

He mouthed, "I want you to ride!"

Walking towards the tub, Carla let him get in first; it Would be easier to use him as a balance if he was already in the water. Without further ado, she straddled him. The invasion of his instrument sliding between the lips of her vagina, reminded them both of what a long week it had been. Carla felt as if she merely existed during the week until she reunited with Joshua on Friday's. In that moment, when he cradled her hips as he embraced her, that's when she felt alive. She swore there was fire in his touch- a sedative that shut down her mind, but made her body naturally respond.

Both sated from their lovemaking, Carla laid into Joshua's embrace. He was quiet, but that wasn't anything unusual. Her fingers outlined his hand print on her stomach and the baby moved gently under his fingers. No matter how many children Joshua had, he never took the gift of life for granted. His only regret was that he hadn't made more out of his life, hadn't made his children make more out of their lives.

His twin daughter and son, Jayden and Jayla were thieves. His other daughter, Jasmine, was Dre's girlfriend and a reformed porn star and he couldn't forget about his gay son. Jonathan, who was...was...well... shit, he was just too fucking weird for Joshua to handle. His sexual preference was fine, but the wigs, costume jewelry and make-up, had done a number on Joshua's stomach. The truth was that his son wasn't a pretty woman, at all. But here he was with Carla and a second chance to get it right with this baby. He forced her to lay back against him with a slight shove to the side of her head so that he could have access to her neck. With slow, deliberate kisses, he felt her body completely relax and after a few silent minutes, he was ready:

"My mother wasn't a crack whore - she didn't do drugs, she didn't drink hard liquor, and she barely drank wine. She was a hood soldier, one hundred and ten percent. My father wasn't around and she worked day and night to keep a roof over our head, but I was bad as fuck. I don't remember a day that went by that I hadn't given her the blues by the time I had turned twelve. I didn't intentionally become mischievous, but it was easier than being good. It started when I had my first taste of coochie. I thought I was the man. No one could tell me anything. I was eleven, she was sixteen."

He heard Carla gasp, but he continued. "I wasn't your average eleven year old, I was already 5'6" and I was well endowed, even back then. Barbie is what we called her. She was my babysitter three nights a week, and God how I loved when she watched me. She'd come over in one outfit, but halfway through the night she'd change. At first her advances were subtle; she would wear booty shorts and a colorful tank top to match. Her hair was combed and she always smelled nice. One night, we were clowning around, I bumped into her and she spilled her pop on her clothes. I mean the way I saw it, it was an ample opportunity for her. She undressed in front of me, walked over and said, "See what you made me do?" Then she walked passed me to the wash room."

Joshua paused and Carla shifted so that she could partially look at him and whispered, "I'm listening Baby, keep going." For the first time, he was letting her in. He was exposing a part of him that he'd been able to hide and if it took them all night, she'd allow him to finish his story.

"Watching her walk around the house in just panties and bra had my hormones raging. I had already experienced my first wet dream. Me and Moms had already talked about it, but the real thing was something totally different. So when she walked back past me, I slapped her on the ass. Barbie turned around and lifted her eyebrow with a smirk on her lips, and at that moment, I knew that she understood the game. She walked towards me like a cat in heat and said, "Do it again!" Now me being nothing, but a horn ball, I was game. We went to my room, she set the tone and I followed. I pulled the condoms out that Moms had given me, she put it on me and by it being my first time, she rode. She slid down my shaft and I wasn't sure what it was suppose to feel like, but God did it feel good."

Joshua paused when Carla lifted up to let the water out of the tub and began running fresh, warm water. She assumed they wouldn't be going anywhere for a while. When she laid back against him, he continued:

"After the first time, we made it a ritual. Each encounter Barbie would show me something different, she'd let me feel on different parts of her body. Show me how to make her cum with my hands and then how to properly stroke her to bring the most satisfaction. She explained that all women were different, but pleasure was a common denominator. She advised that I work on my game in order to be able to please any kind of woman. Some wanted it rough, some liked it slow, and some were just fucking kinky. So she upped the bid on the game. She had this friend that was just as fine, just as sexy and just as freaky as her. She wanted me to execute everything she'd taught me on her while she watched. Her name was Lola."

Carla wanted to tell him that he could spare her with the names, because it sounded more like cartoon porn than anything. *Barbie and Lola*, was Ken going to show up next? What in the hell? Much to her discomfort, she remained silent, he was the narrator.

"After watching for a while, she decided to join in. They would kiss and touch and then they'd start kissing and touching on me. Needless to say that my appetite for women had grown, immensely; knowing that they gained as much satisfaction from me as I gained from them only made me cockier. So I pressed my luck. I started hanging out in the streets with older guys. Shit, I figured that I was getting play just like they were, so that bought me rights to hang with them. Since I wasn't old enough to get a real job, I needed to keep my condom supply plentiful. By no means were Barbie and Lola laying off. Not before long, the streets were talking and somehow the information landed right in Moms lap. And unfortunately for me, she wasn't having it. She shipped my ass off to Grandpa. She figured I needed some guidance and tougher love, but Grandpa wasn't any better." Joshua laughed at the flash back.

Carla smiled as she felt the rumble in Joshua's chest. It was a rare occasion when he laughed so she relished in every opportunity that presented itself.

"Man, Grandpa's old dirty ass was the first person to take me to the strip club. The rules in the house were simple: 1. Don't bring no hoes home 2. Don't get caught with your pants down. 3. Don't bring home hoes with babies. But, I got caught up and by the time I hit fifteen, the twins were on the way… Mom was furious. Grandpa was disappointed, nevertheless he didn't trip, but he made sure that I knew that they were my responsibility. So I got this job at the grocery store as a bagger, but that was a bust. I would have made more money hustling in the streets, but then again, I didn't want that kind of heat. With a twenty-two year old babymama, I didn't feel a need to work extra hard because she worked too. But, I didn't wanna be a dead beat dad like my own pops."

Carla could see Joshua using hand gestures on each side of her, slightly splashing water. It seemed like he was trying to make peace with his past decisions or rationalize them, but either way she would remain silent.

"One night in my room I kept thinking about how Barbie had told me, "The dick was good enough to pay for it." So I did what came naturally. I started charging hoes who wanted to fuck. Some of them paid top dollar, some of them paid per round, but either way they all paid. After a couple of months, I ran into a client who knew someone who ran an underground operation of escorts. She recommended me, therefore I allowed the owner to test me out." Carla raised her eyebrows at the visual picture that she hadn't asked for. "For fifteen years that's what I did. It wasn't my intentions to stay in it so long, but I got caught in the luxury that the life afforded."

"But it wasn't who you were, at least not who you wanted to be, right?" Carla concluded.

"Naw." Joshua's voice softened. "When Grandpa got sick, he made me promise to get my shit together and it took me some time to get out, but I did. Grandpa's been gone for twelve years, moms been gone for eight years and I've been on the straight and narrow for the past ten years. I got a college degree, a decent job with good benefits and then I got you and it seems that God is giving me him." Joshua slightly squeezed Carla's stomach and the baby kicked his hand instead this time. "Maybe God's giving me another chance to be a better parent."

Mistakenly leaving the blinds open over night, the sun shined brightly into Carla's face. Joshua who hadn't moved a muscle was hiding behind her frame and she immediately regretted debating for the side closest to the window. The rumble of her stomach was as strong as the snoring that vibrated off the walls. After twenty minutes of just laying there, Carla decided that she was hungry and when she headed towards the bathroom she heard Joshua groan as the light hit his eyes. Laughing to herself, she figured that he was getting what he deserved.

Breakfast was scrumptious, omelets and pancakes were Carla's absolute favorite. She started to doze off a bit when the car slowed and Joshua pulled into the driveway of a brick two-family flat. Despite the year it was built, it seemed to be in great condition. Joshua turned off the engine and made his way around to open Carla's door. She got out without question, which was rare for her, but she trusted him, so she decided to follow his lead.

As they approached the front door, Joshua took the key out of his pocket and put it in the front door when Carla couldn't hold back the curiosity any further. "Whose house is this?"

Joshua gave her the side-eye because he had been waiting for the questions since he pulled in the driveway. He knew her ass was nosey by nature, but he accepted it. "It's my house, well Grandpa's house. I bought it for him about fifteen years ago." Pushing the door open, Carla expected to see dust everywhere, a few spiders and coca bugs, but it was spotless.

"How does it stay so clean?" She questioned some more.

"I cleaned it the last time I was here?"

"When you came to see Vanessa?" Carla concluded.

Joshua was silent for a few minutes. "Yes, when I came to see Vanessa. The cleaning helped clear my mind."

"Are you still struggling with that?" She asked as carefully as possible.

"Have you ever seen a dead baby in a casket?" The weariness that he silently dealt with became evident on his face.

"No, but I know what it's like to feel that kind of loss. I didn't have to hold my baby in my arms to have an expectation of its arrival. But, I'm familiar with the feeling of having it snatched away from me." She quietly stated.

Joshua was careful about what he said to Carla, he remembered that she had suffered a loss as well. "Sometimes, well most times…" He decided to be honest, hoping that it would free his conscious. "When I'm at the house in Chicago, I dream. I can see her clear as day- she's in the casket and I can hear Vanessa crying and I can remember not dropping one tear. She was flesh of my flesh and blood of my blood, yet I felt nothing."

Carla wrapped her arms around him and she whispered in his ear, "That doesn't make you a bad person; you didn't know that she existed, you hadn't been waiting on her arrival." Carla rubbed the crown of his head to soothe him. "You're a good man for seeing to it that things were settled before you moved along."

"I get it, but it still doesn't make me feel any better." Joshua argued.

"What would make it better for you? What would help ease the pain of what you feel?" Carla probed.

"That, I'm not sure of!" Joshua answered honestly.

"Have you talked to Vanessa lately?" She continued to question him as she wondered from room to room.

"I checked on her a few weeks ago." He confessed with his hands clenched in his pockets.

"Do you think you need to check on her while you're here?" Carla seemed to wonder aimlessly, but her heart was pounding faster by the second. She didn't want to make such a suggestion, but she knew it was the right thing to do. When Joshua remained silent, she said, "I can remain in the car, as long as you remain on the porch." She knew the ultimatum was petty, but the words *dumb, stupid* or *naïve* were not written across her forehead. It wasn't that she didn't trust Joshua, but she comprehended what predicaments vulnerability could place anyone in.

"We don't have to go!"

"But, it seems like you need to!" Carla encouraged.

"I got a few more stops to make, let's go." He urged.

Carla walked back towards the front door and Joshua locked up behind them. The further they drove the rougher the neighborhood got. "Where are we now?"

"It's a small town I grew up in called Aliquippa."

"Ali what?" Carla scrunched her face.

Laughing, he repeated the word as he skillfully pulled in between two cars, "Ali-quip-pa."

The bar was across from the police station and there were all kinds of individuals that parlayed around the front of the building. Carla wasn't sure if she should leave her purse in the car or bring it with her. Almost reading her mind, Joshua said, "Leave the purse in the car, you won't need it in here."

She reached for his hand, "You got us right?"

"I got you, I'd never put you in harms way. You wanted to know about me, I just wanted to show you." Joshua caressed her face.

Without another word, Carla got out of the car and came around to join hands with Joshua. The closer they moved towards the door of the bar, the more she heard the word "Ice" floating in the air. She tried to shake off the agitation; it wasn't worth interrupting the healing that was taking place for Joshua. He needed to come back here, he needed to have the approval and acceptance from Carla- that he was good enough for her and her family and when the trip was over he'd have it.

"Oh the Ice-Man cometh." The bartender announced and every head in the bar turned.

"Aye, cut that out. I just came in here to have a beer and play a game of pool with my lady." Joshua gestured towards Carla and she extended her hand to the bartender when his larger one swallowed hers. "Noah, Carla. Carla, Noah."

"She sure is pretty on the eyes, Ice." He leaned over the counter and smiled. "A pretty pregnant one too, huh?"

"Chill-out." Joshua laughed, Noah wasn't exactly what he'd call tactful. "Give me a Miller and the balls to the table." He looked over at Carla, "You got time for a game?"

"Do you have time to be spanked? That's the real question." She smiled, knowing that she had played her share of pool in her day.

Joshua figured he'd go easy on her when he allowed her to break, but when three of the stripped balls went into the three separate pockets on the first try, he regretted his decision. "Oh so you can play?" He smugly questioned.

"Baby, I tried to tell you." Carla innocently blinked her eyes at him.

Joshua took a swig of his beer and attempted to catch up. They rotated four turns and the game was over. Of course Joshua won, but he considered Carla to be a worthy opponent. It was a stroke of luck that he got the eight ball in the same pocket that he said he would on the first try, or else, Carla would have won. He pulled her to his side and kissed her lips. "You cease to amaze me!"

Her eyelids fluttered a bit, public display of affection from him in a place where he had a reputation to uphold made her weak, "I love you, Babe."

He rubbed his nose against hers, "I love you too. Let's get out of here."

Crossing over the threshold, Carla brushed shoulders with a woman - well at least she thought it was a woman. She went to say excuse me and came face to face with a very butch looking female. The only thing that gave her away were the D cup breasts that she wasn't about to hide underneath the baggy, manly clothing.

When Joshua turned around to address the hold up, he smiled while gesturing towards the woman. "Aww Baby, say it ain't so!"

"Ice-Baby, what it do?" The woman chimed.

Joshua hugged the woman longer than Carla would have expected. "Aww sweetie, it's been much too long."

"I know, we miss you around here!" The woman confessed.

"It's certainly good to be missed." Joshua returned the confession.

"Have you talked to that nephew of mine?" She inquired while lightly punching him in the shoulder.

"I can't lie, I haven't. You?"

"Naw, the last I heard he was still out here on the prowl. Y'all need to squash it, Ice." The woman scolded.

"There's no beef Shay, he's going to always be my son. Nothing or no one can change that."

Slowly, Carla was piecing the information together. *Looks like homosexuality runs in the family*, she thought to herself.

Reading the thoughts in her mind again, Joshua reached for Carla's hand. "Shay-Baby, this is my girlfriend and the mother of another unborn Reed, Carla. Carla, this is Jonathan's aunty, Shay!"

"Well aren't you a pretty piece of pussy!" Shay complimented.

Carla couldn't help but blush at her vulgarity. "Well how sweet of you, thank you!"

Joshua shook his head, he'd never been able to get Shay to watch her mouth. He figured it was no point in correcting her now. "I hate we don't have more time, but we've got to keep in touch." Joshua took Shay's phone that was clutched in her hand and placed his number in it. "Call me," He paused. "For anything." He hugged her again, kissed her cheek and they were off in the direction of his truck.

Settled in her seat, Carla asked. "When's the last time you saw Jonathan?"

"It's been a long while Baby." He adjusted the rearview mirror so that he could see his reflection. "A long while." He'd come from *this...here*, yet he had survived.

Back at the hotel, Carla soaked in the tub and Joshua packed their luggage. He intended to be back on the road by checkout, he'd have Carla tucked away in bed by 6pm at the latest.

"So I guess we could redecorate Grandpa's house to add our own flavor. Pittsburgh would be an adjustment, but the baby and I could get used to it."

"What are you talking about Baby?" Joshua walked over towards the tub.

"Isn't that why we're here? You said we'd have to leave once the baby got here because of all that stuff with Dre."

"Baby, we're not moving. I've already talked to Dre."

She stopped lathering her towel with soap. "You talked to him? When?"

"After your last doctor's appointment. We talked. I gave him back the money, my lawyer showed up along with a few additional legal officials. It's done. We're good, it's over." Joshua's hands moved like he was a disc jockey.

"And he's just supposed to drop it, just like that?" She snapped her fingers for dramatic purposes.

"It's done, just like that." He mimicked her snap.

She smiled at his sarcasm, but she wasn't at ease. If no one knew Dre, she did. It wasn't over, not by a long shot.

CHAPTER 14

Residue

$\mathcal{M}$ organ rolled over and simply stared at her alarm clock. The level of irritation that rose with her should have been completely illegal because it was deadly and dangerous. She wasn't feeling well and it was starting to effect her behavior. The medicine that the doctor had prescribed was supposed to help with the nausea, but either he was lying or her body was rejecting it. Yet, the whole process seemed extremely weird, because it was rare that she ever got sick.

Morgan didn't know how she was going to make it through the day. Although, she was thankful for the peacefulness between her and her husband, not even he could rescue her from the bullshit that lay ahead. There were whiners, complainers, suicide attempts, the rich, the spoiled and the insane. Now don't get it wrong, there were plenty of her clients that actually needed her help and utilized her counsel. But half of these mothafuckas were just down right crazy and the other half seriously needed Jesus.

It was Morgan's job to decipher who was there for help and who was there for show. There were some patients who wanted a stress leave from work and sincerely needed it and then there were others who just wanted a few weeks at the crib. Nonetheless, she obliged but in moderation. For some she'd give two weeks rather than a month and sometimes it frankly depended on her mood. Just like her patients needed a break from work, she too needed a break.

Morgan felt the bile rise in her throat again and wondered when her vacation time was scheduled for. She couldn't resist some R& R, but then again, rest and relaxation was what had gotten her into this situation.

After thirty minutes of non movement, Brandon walked back into the room towards Morgan's side of the bed. "Baby, I know you don't feel well, but if you're going to work today then you'd better get a move on it."

Her only reply was a moan.

"What time is the Dr.'s appointment today?"

"12:30." Morgan mumbled.

"I'll meet you there by 12:20, okay?"

"I think we should just cancel the appointment, Babe. Can't you just lay here with me for a little while longer?" Morgan whined.

"Baby." He breathed while rubbing her face. "The doctor said that it was important, we can't cancel and plus you need to ask him about this rash that you have. You've been scratching it for almost a week." Brandon pulled Morgan's legs from under the cover and helped her make her way to the bathroom before running out the door. He had court in thirty minutes and he couldn't be late.

Dragging her feet towards the entrance of the private practice, she tried to brace herself. She had a new client and she had given herself an hour to prepare. First impressions were always the most permanent impressions and not giving a fuck wasn't the impression that she wanted to display. Although, she was very close to just throwing in the towel, closing the business and spending her time curled up in her bed with her man or a good book with a sexy man in it.

The coffee slid down her throat and warmed her, but it did nothing to help settle her stomach. Morgan was just about to buzz her secretary when there was a knock at her door before it was gently pushed open. "Good Morning Dr. Morrison, your client is here." The secretary announced.

Morgan waited the few seconds as the secretary stepped aside and the client entered the room, but as Carla's face brightened at seeing her best friend, Morgan's seemed to dim. "What are you doing here girl? I have an appointment in a few minutes." Morgan told her.

"Uh hello, I am the appointment."

"Really? Do you actually plan to pay me for the advice that I'm going to give you today?"

Slightly insulted, Carla reassured, "Your secretary ran my insurance, it seems to be covered."

"Ohhh this must be serious." Morgan sat down in her chair. "Cause you're here, in my office, and you paid."

"I believe that confidentiality has a price." Carla was learning that people were still people at the end of the day and that valuable information was the key to any gossip session.

"Oh that it does." Morgan felt a bit of tension in the room. "Should I be offended that you didn't trust me as a friend to talk?"

"It's not that, it's just that it's sensitive information that I will sue your rich a--, self." Carla corrected herself. "I will sue your rich self if you breach it." Carla informed.

"Alright, well let's get started."

"Before we do that, are you alright? You look a bit flushed." Carla noticed.

"I'm okay, I haven't been feeling well, but it's probably just a virus." Morgan wasn't sure why she lied, but it just seemed to be the right thing to do. Besides, they weren't there to talk about her.

"Alright, well lets get started then. I'm assuming that I go first?" Carla asked.

"Certainly, what brought you here today?"

"So Joshua and I had a wonderful weekend together in Pennsylvania. I learned a lot about him, he shared some personal things with me about his childhood, which I'm grateful for, but now I have some concerns."

"Such as?" Dr. Morgan was well into her role.

"Such as the amount of women that he's been with. It's not something that we've discussed in detail, but I'm intelligent enough to know that ya boy don been around the world and seen a lot of places – walls in particular. And I'm just not sure how that makes me feel."

"Well from your inability to take a breath in between sentences, you're antsy in your chair and your hand gestures are all over the place, it seems to me that it makes you a bit uncomfortable. Almost as if you're trying to find peace with the situation, but there is none."

"I think that the information Joshua shared with me made me feel a little insecure. I mean he's had ménage à trois', old women, young women, married women, single women, black women, white women…"

Morgan held up her hand. "He's very diverse in his taste, I see."

"Don't use that fu--," Carla caught herself again." Don't use that condescending tone with me. It was his job, he was a…a…a male escort in a certain period of his life." Carla stammered. It was the first time since she found out that she had let such a secret roll off of her tongue.

The only response that Carla received from Morgan was a lifted eyebrow. Just as she was about to write something on the pad that she positioned in her lap, Carla snatched it and said, "This is a very confidential meeting, no notes will be necessary and/or allowed."

When Morgan slowly nodded, Carla smiled. "Good, now that we understand each other, tell me what I should do!"

"Tell you what to do?" Morgan questioned. "I don't believe that you've rendered a problem that should be offered a solution."

Understanding her point, Carla tried to swing it another way. "His former life makes me insecure. It doesn't make me love him any less. It makes me sorry for him, that he felt that was the only option available to him. But, now I can't help feeling that he's had better than me- that my love making is simply mediocre."

Crossing her left leg over her right, Morgan felt a slight headache approaching, her clock assured her in about thirty minutes her professional day would be concluding. "In my professional opinion..." She paused to gather her thoughts as her nausea seemed to climb a step closer to the back of her throat. "I believe that simple communication will do the trick. Not only are you emotional in this stage of your pregnancy, but you've gained some weight, you're vulnerable and what you need is reassurance."

"Reassurance?" Carla questioned.

"Yes, reassurance that you and the baby are enough for him. Reassurance that there are only two people in your bedroom and reassurance that the love that you have to offer him will be enough to mend what's broken in him." Morgan concluded.

"I mean that could work, and trust me, I'm not doubting your skills, but Joshua is another kind of animal." Carla half smiled, half laughed. "He's certainly not human and what you're proposing is so much easier said than done."

"Ok. Let's try another approach." Morgan began, "Has he mentioned your weight gain?"

"No."

"Has he mentioned your sex game?"

"No."

"Head game?"

"No."

"Has he mentioned areas that you could improve?" Morgan continued.

"No."

"Does he hold you after love making?"

"Always." Carla smiled.

"Good. Then in my professional opinion, I'd like to say that you're conjuring these emotions up in your head. Until the man gives you a reason to make you feel inadequate, simply pray about how you feel. You don't want to make an issue out of him confiding in you. For now, just let it go." Morgan got up and moved towards her desk. "Go home and love on your man."

"Okay, but who said I was done? Why are you packing up your things?" Carla was annoyed.

"Sweetie Pie, your paid session ended ten minutes ago. If you need to reschedule another appointment the secretary is in the hallway."

"I hope wherever you're headed, they have some kind of medical utensil to pull your head out of your anus."

"Aww fuck you." Morgan smiled. "Yes, I said fuck you, now get your pregnant ass out of my office and continue to expound upon your newfound vocabulary. While you're improving your language, I plan to use every dirty word I know, every fucking chance I get. Can I get an Amen?"

Carla laughed. "You're going to hell, dude."

"I know you'll save me a seat!" Morgan smooched in the air.

"I won't be there, but I can talk to your mama about saving you one."

"You dirty dog." Morgan laughed.

"I'll see you Saturday at your house. Don't forget the girls will be there to set up for the shower early." Carla waved and walked out the door.

"Oh, shit the shower." Morgan mumbled.

Approximately twelve minutes later, Morgan pulled into her doctor's office parking lot and took a few minutes to exhale. She had been trying to avoid thinking about what the doctor could possibly need to see them regarding. However, she was as ready as she was going to be. Getting out of the car, dragging her feet towards the door, Morgan found herself signing in and having a seat next to the stand of magazines for expecting mothers. She felt so drained, as if someone had borrowed that last bit of energy that she had saved.

Looking at her watch, she wasn't sure that Brandon was going to make it. Just as her name was called, he walked through the door. He had literally just saved his own ass, because she had planned to tag it if he had missed this appointment.

Following the doctor into his office, rather than into an examination room threw Morgan for a loop. When she sat in the chair and waited for the doctor to elaborate on the visit, her nerves stretched closer to the edge.

"If I'm correct in my calculations Mrs. Morrison, you're about nine weeks pregnant, correct?"

Morgan looked at Brandon, "That's correct."

"How do you feel, so far?"

"I've just been really tired. A little crampy, but I expect that it's normal with my body going through so many changes to accommodate the baby." Morgan looked at Brandon again, who had grabbed her hand.

"And then she's got this rash, she's a little more pale than usual." Brandon hesitated. "Is that a part of the pregnancy process as well?"

"Can I see the rash?" The doctor put on some gloves and leaned over to take a look at Morgan's arm. "No it's not a part of the pregnancy." At least not in Morgan's case, he thought to himself. "Morgan, your white blood count is extremely low. I ran some test's from your urine and blood from the last time that you were here and the results were abnormal."

"Okay, so what does that mean?"

"With what I can gather so far, I believe that you have Lupus. The rash and the paleness are just some symptoms. Do you mind if I take your temperature?"

"Okay, but what does my temperature have to do with anything?"

Taking the thermometer out and sticking it under her tongue, gave the doctor the momentary silence he needed. It was hard explaining things like this to patients, but he had more to share. "101.2, you have a fever. I believe you're in the process of having a flare."

"Okay, hold on." She looked at her husband wearily." What does all of this mean? Flares? Rashes?" One hand was secured in Brandon's and the other was wailing in the air.

"Lupus is an autoimmune disease." The doctor faltered when he realized that she wasn't following him. "It's when the body begins to fight with itself, the cells begin to fight each other and the main targets are your joints. It doesn't seem that you're experiencing any joint pain as of yet, but that doesn't mean that the fetus' joints, heart and kidneys won't have issues."

Squeezing her husband's hand, Morgan questioned, "Wait, so Lupus affects pregnancy?"

"Very much so, I'm afraid."

"But, how did I get it?"

"It's very unexplainable." The doctor began, "Sometimes it's genetic and it could have been laying dormant, which means that it could have been in remission. Or, this pregnancy could have triggered it with all the changes that your body seems to be going through. And sometimes it just happens. It varies from person to person, but I'd like to continue more tests and see what alternatives we can find."

"So what happens now?" Feeling defeated, Morgan asked.

"There isn't a cure for it, but there is medication that can control it."

"But will it harm my baby?" Brandon spoke up.

"It's very possible that you will not be able to carry this baby to term. Miscarriages occur because it's the body's way of saying that something is not normal and it needs to get rid of it. But, if you do carry the baby to term, it is likely that there will be some birth defects that will cause permanent damage to the fetus' mobile activity."

Brandon pulled out his phone and at first thought to text Carla for some assistance, but he knew that Carla was probably the last person that his wife wanted to see. They didn't need the aggravation of Carla's pregnancy at this time. So, he texted his brother and asked him to come and drive Morgan's car home. At this point, she was in no condition to drive. She looked as if she was going to vomit.

Exiting the office doors, Morgan was numb. She didn't hear anything else that was explained to her. She hadn't confirmed yes or no on the medication, she hadn't shaken the doctors hand once he offered it and she barely felt her husband's presence beside her. Her world was shaken. She couldn't begin to think about what she had done to deserve to be dealt such a hand. She prayed regularly, she attended services every Sunday, she tithed every check faithfully and somehow she'd gotten screwed.

Sitting beside her, Brandon reached over and kissed her cheek, "It's going to be okay, we're going to figure this out." Morgan couldn't bring herself to reply, she just couldn't.

Walking into the house, Brandon acknowledged the babysitter who had been instructed to pick Skylar up from school. He needed more quiet time with his wife before he could begin to deal with his daughter, because his wife was in no condition to do so.

Brandon made his way to their master bathroom and began running warm water as he watched Morgan sit lifeless on the bed. He saw it in her eyes, she had given up. As he slowly undressed her, Brandon kissed her cheeks and her neck, as he promised that he'd make everything better. He initially thought she hadn't heard him, but the tears that rolled down her face were evidence that she had.

Easing her into the water, he urged her to just relax. He went in search of her cell phone and tablet – getting in touch with her secretary, he asked that she call all clients and reschedule all appointments that were scheduled within the next seventy-two hours. His wife needed a break and some down time, so he internally agreed to do the same. He called one of the partners and advised that he needed to take a family leave for the rest of the week- nothing was more important than his wife and her emotional stability at the moment.

CHAPTER 15

Thou Shall Not Test Me!

*A*fter a long day of catering the event of a sweet sixteen birthday party for a spoiled brat, whose parents continued to reference her as a pretty princess, Ebony's nerves were shot. The little girl had cried and demanded, yelled and then cried some more until every detail was to her liking. If the parents hadn't paid Ebony five thousand dollars for her services, on top of supplies and travel, she would have graciously told them all to kiss her ass. She solemnly swore that Amber would never act in such a manner that was borderline tyrant and disrespectful.

The only thing that Ebony wanted to do was grab some wine, soak in the tub and make love to her husband. Entering the front door, she found Ivan sitting with his legs crossed, the lights off and the television muted. Ebony's immediate reaction was concern, "What's going on, Babe?" When he didn't answer, she repeated the question.

Instead of a response, Ivan slid the package across the table. It wasn't often that something could rock his mood, so Ebony was cautious.

"They served me with this, since you weren't home." Ivan disclosed.

Ebony picked up the envelope and screeched, "I can't believe this bastard." Looking at her husband and seeing the weariness in his eyes. "I don't even know what to say, Babe."

"I called Brandon to see if they handle this kind of thing and to explore some options." Ivan looked in Ebony's expecting eyes. "It's no use, Babe, he has rights."

She screeched louder this time, "And what the fuck am I suppose to tell our daughter? Ugh, the balls on this, bitch."

Ivan rubbed his hands together. "You'll have to tell her that I'm not her biological father."

"Bullshit, blood couldn't make that sentence more bullshit. You're her father and I'll show my whole ass before I allow anyone to take that from you!" Ebony headed up the stairs of their home with Ivan calling behind her. When she returned, she had changed into some jeans and gym shoes. She walked passed Ivan and into the kitchen where she began boiling a pot of water and when it finished, she poured it into a large thermos container.

Ebony scooped up the bat that she kept in the corner while Ivan had been away from home, due to their estrangement, and she walked out the door. Ivan yelled her name from the front door and Ebony yelled back over her shoulder, "I'll be back babe, no worries."

Putting her car in park as she reached the ranch styled-brick home. Ebony grabbed the jug and tucked the bat under her arm. She thought about calling her sisters, but they would only make it worse. Walking to the front porch and ringing the doorbell, Ebony began asking God for forgiveness for what she was bout to do. Then she said, "Forgive him father, for he knows not what he has done." She wasn't wrong for her actions; the bible said that if you have an issue with your brother then go to him. Well, here she was.

As the locks turned, Ebony tightened her hand on the arm of the bat. When Antoine's mother appeared in the doorway, Ebony greeted, "Good Morning Judy." She pushed her body in the house, forcing Judy to step back. "Where's your son?" Judy hesitated and Ebony headed for the stairs.

"Please Ebony, he's sleeping and he's had a long day." Judy pleaded.

"Well Sweetie, it is about to get a little longer." Ebony replied without breaking her stride, she climbed the stairs two at a time to give herself more time to address him. She knew how Judy worked, Antoine was a mama's boy, and she knew that she had about ten minutes before the police showed up. It wasn't the first time that she had to show out and it wasn't going to be the last.

Standing over his sleeping body, Ebony briefly watched his chest rise and fall. She unscrewed the top of the thermos and stuck two fingers in it to ensure that it was still pretty hot. And without hesitation she splashed it all over him, dousing him like a hot shower. When Antoine jumped up, gasping for air, Ebony hit him in the thigh with the bat starting with the left side and then mimicking the motion on his right side. He tried to turn to avoid the swing and then she tagged his ass again.

"You dirty mother fucker." She only pronounced her words when she was really pissed. She needed the opponent to feel her rage. "You had me served?" She continued to swing the bat, but by now he was wide awoke and a little quicker in dodging. "You want custody of my daughter bitch? Then bring it."

He caught the bat mid swing and pulled her against his chest. "Stop it. You told me that you'd only let me see her in court, so I did exactly what you asked, now stop it."

"Go to hell. If I can help it, you'll never see her. She doesn't know you and I don't particularly care for her to. She has a father."

"Yes she does, me!" Antoine shouted.

Ebony slapped his face faster than he could stop her. "According to her birth certificate, it's him. He was the one that was there. He took responsibility for her, he raised her. So before your retarded self thinks about being disrespectful again, I'd tread lightly if I were you." She walked out of the door and headed for the front door, while ranting. "Fucking Pillsbury Doughboy looking ass."

Sitting back behind the wheel of her car, Ebony was still fuming. She called Chrissey who answered on the second ring and asked her to call Carla on three-way. When all three sisters were on the line, Ebony cut loose, "That nicca don lost his mind y'all."

"Who?" Chrissey asked.

"Antoine had Ivan and I served with custody papers today."

Chrissey whistled, "Oh that fat bitch got balls."

Ebony rolled her eyes as if they could see her. "Too bad he ain't got dick."

"Wait, he got a little peter?" Carla questioned.

Ebony laughed, "Dawg, God must have been busy giving all the big peters to all the little men cause I swear they got hella hang."

"I promise I thought it was just me." Chrissey joined in with her. "I mean I keep a fat nicca with a big ding-a-ling, but baaabyyyy every now and then I get me a short skinny one and honey be hung like a horse.

"Neigh. Neigh." Carla joined in, making horse noises.

Laughing at their stupidity, they'd done it again, Ebony thought. Her sisters were simply incredible, her pressure was back in check and now she was ready to go home. "I'll tell you what though…"

"What's that?" Carla asked.

"I did a good job of beating that ass with a bat." She boasted.

"Good, that slick Will, lil dick, Alfalfa looking jerk better be lucky that you left the clip at home this time." Chrissey went in.

Ebony gasped, "Carla told you about that?"

Chrissey smacked her lips, "Of course she did, but the real question is, why didn't you tell me?" She checked.

"I meant too, we just haven't had a minute to talk." Ebony tried to reassure her.

"Hmm mmm." Chrissey said as she disconnected the call.

Ebony entered the house with Ivan sitting in the same position that she found him in when she originally came home from work. She held her hand up to stop him from asking. "I need a bath and some wine." She moved closer to him. "Where's Amber?"

"Brandon called and asked if she could come over and play with Skylar. Ya know, keep each other company."

"Oh!" She smiled. "So it's just you and I?"

He pulled her into his lap. "Yes, it's just you and I. I have a few things in mind."

She lowered her mouth to his. "Please Mr. Johnson, have your way with me." For the time being she pushed everything else out of her mind. Ebony planned to join that bastard idiot in court. She was a Williams and they fought fire with fire. Well a former Williams, as of now, she was Mrs. Johnson, Mrs. Ivan Johnson.

CHAPTER 16

An Illusion Of Reality!

$\mathcal{C}$ hrissey saw the crowd of people running, she saw his mouth moving, but she couldn't hear the words coming from his lips. It wasn't until she heard the gunshots ring out and his body fall to the ground that she felt the wind being snatched from her chest. As she fell to her knees, Chrissey sensed the life leave his body. She never thought in her wildest dreams that he'd leave her. She could only remember screaming, "Oh God, please, no!"

Chrissey felt someone touch her shoulder and squeeze, but no one was standing over her. It wasn't until she felt as if she was being pulled down and suffocated that she woke up swinging. Ebony was calling her name and yelling for her to wake up. Chrissey's face was drenched as she continued to squeal.

"It was so real." Chrissey whispered out of breath.

"What was real?" Ebony asked mortified.

"The dream. Daniel got killed and I was crying and screaming." Chrissey said as she wiped her face.

"Looks like you were really crying and yelling and not just in the dream." Ebony examined. "And you overslept, you were suppose to meet me at Morgan's house two hours ago. The shower starts in two hours." Ebony gently reminded.

"Oh my God, okay give me ten minutes." Chrissey scrambled to her feet.

"You are going to wash up, aren't you?" Ebony raised her eyebrows.

Chrissey gave Ebony the side eye. In some cases she might of skipped the cleansing process, but not today. Today she was going to have to engage with too many people. "Of course I am, jerk!"

"I'm just checking. Make sure you get the crack of that ass real good too." Ebony laughed.

"I'll be sure to let you inspect it once I'm done, alright?"

Shrugging her shoulders and giving her sister the middle finger. "I'll do whatever needs to be done to ensure that you do it right." Ebony assured.

As guests begin to arrive, Ebony and Chrissey did a last minute check of everything. The cake table was flawlessly decorated with candy that color coordinated with the scheme of the cake. Every table had center pieces, there were blue, green and yellow balloons everywhere and accented decorations to match. The little prince would be making his entrance in about eight weeks and his royal parents would be arriving in eight minutes. They wanted everything to go off without any hiccups.

Watching Brandon stroll past them as he headed back into the house, Chrissey stopped him, "Is everything alright with Morgan, we haven't seen her much during the set up process?"

"She hasn't been feeling well, so she's lying down." He informed.

"Is everything alright?" Ebony asked concerned.

Brandon wasn't one to lie because he didn't lie very well, so he offered them the only bit of truth that he could. "It will be. Let me know if you guys need anything else." And with that he made his way back towards the house.

In honor of the baby shower being hosted at the Morrison's home, they provided the catering as well as waitstaff for the guests. The sisters weren't sure how well Carla was going to take the news that Morgan was sitting out on her special day, but they would try to keep her as occupied as possible.

The sound of whistles and screams came from the other side of the room, signaling Chrissey and Ebony that it was show time. Just as Chrissey was going in search of the first game to be played, James grabbed her by the elbow to grasp her attention.

"Miss. Williams, it's a pleasure as always."

"I'd like to say the same, but your ass just keeps popping up and without an invitation." Chrissey insulted.

"Oh, but I was invited." He assured.

"By who?" Chrissey questioned.

"By me." They both turned towards the voice and Chrissey cringed. Carlos had a way of interfering that caused one to go in hiding.

"Oh, how nice of you daddy, you two enjoy each other." Chrissey held her smile in place as she walked off. Later, she'd require an explanation from her father. She was sure that his reply was going to be that it was the leading of the Holy Spirit. "Bullshit, this is totally bullshit."

The gift table was over capacity. The music from the DJ had everyone on the dance floor and the food had been just as filling as it was scrumptious. Everything was going as planned when Carla stepped in Ebony's path. "Hey, where's Morgan? I haven't seen her all day!"

"Brandon said that she wasn't feeling well and was upstairs sleeping." Ebony labored her breathing. She knew this moment was coming; it was simply a matter of time.

"Really?" Carla wasn't buying it, this was an important day for her. It was one step under getting married and she hadn't missed either event when it had been Morgan's turn. Something smelled fishy and she was determined to get to the bottom of it. But, she'd hold off until the guests were gone. She wouldn't dare make it seem as though she hadn't been grateful for those that had taken time out of their day to spend it with her and Joshua.

Carla felt him before he wrapped his arms around her. Joshua seemed to sense her storm and tried to calm it before it had the opportunity to progress.

Whispering, Joshua said, "Whatever it is, let it go Sug." She went to protest, but he stopped her. "It's written all over your face." She turned in his arms and before she could address him, he kissed her gently and breathlessly whispered, "Come dance with me!"

She heard the faint sound of Beyoncé's *One Plus One* playing in the background and nodded. But, by the time they finally reached the dance floor, the song had switched to *Rocket* and as if on cue, Ebony appeared with a chair for Joshua to sit in as Carla began to sing:

> *Let me sit this back on ya!*
> *Show you how I feel*
> *Let me take this off*
> *Will you watch me?*
> *That's mass appeal*
> *Don't take your eyes...*
> *Don't take your eyes off it*
> *Watch it..*

> *Babe..*
> *If you like it, you can touch it babe...*
> *Do you wanna touch it babe?*

It was almost like a strip tease, but with their clothes on. Totally inappropriate for a royal baby shower, but, totally appropriate for a Williams' baby shower. After the first chorus, Ebony pulled Ivan to the floor and inevitably Chrissey grabbed James. All three girls were defiant, mischievous and sexual all within their own right. Chrissey's entire body was built with sex appeal- it radiated with it. All she had to do was walk in a room and the atmosphere shifted, noticeably. But the way Ebony's eyes slanted and her eye lashes curved over her eyes had men that she encountered weak at the knees. Yet, Ivan held the mysteries of her intent. Carla on the other hand was different; it was her personality that drew the opposite sex.

Please don't misunderstand though, Carla was the shapeliest of the sisters, she had more curves and body than her two sisters combined. However, she wasn't as fluent in body language. She could move her hips and sway her body, but she wasn't what she considered seductive. It was Carla's smile that intrigued men and then her wit. She handled people with care and exuded a friendliness that made you fall in love with her, and that was a desired trait. Carla was Eileen's sweetest daughter, Ebony was spice, but Chrissey was surely the salt.

Chrissey had the appearance of sugar, oh but once you tasted her, it was hard to get her off your tongue.

When the song ended, Chrissey was still in her feelings about James being present. But she'd take one for the team for the sake of the event. The constant interaction with him throughout the day reminded Chrissey of her lingering dream from that morning. He was a representation that consistently emphasized, *Danger is near.*

Ebony gathered everyone's attention. "Now, here's the best part of this shindig!" Chrissey began positioning the guests of honor chair's in the middle of the dance floor. "It's gift opening time."

Ebony read the cards and Chrissey unwrapped the gifts. The Ohhh's and Ahhh's filled the elegantly decorated backyard. It signified how precious, significant and appreciated each gift received was.

Carla's parents had out-done themselves by purchasing the four way crib that turned into a toddler's bed. The stroller and matching car seat that they purchased reflected the soft baby colors of blue, green and yellow that Carla insisted the shower be. Tomorrow the nursery was scheduled to be completed and since Joshua had to get back on the road, Carla had arranged for someone to put together the crib, dressers and changing table in the baby's room.

Carla had gotten so big that not only did Joshua have to help her veet (rid her body of all of the unnecessary hair) her sensitive areas, but he had helped her get dressed for the shower. Since her bending was limited, he was responsible for putting on her underwear while she kept her balance by holding onto his shoulders; snapping her bra, putting on her pants-when she wore them and setting out her shoes. She had eight more weeks to go and she was ready. The closer she got to the delivery date, the more unreal it still seemed to her!

As the party cleared, Carla had ordered Ivan, Joshua and Brandon about with her specific instructions on how she wanted the gifts arranged in the cars. Keeping them busy gave her time to sneak upstairs and see for herself what was going on with Morgan. Entering the Morrison's master bedroom suite, she caught vision of the sleeping Morgan. Walking towards the bed, she picked up the medicine bottle on the nightstand as she recognized the familiar prescription for nausea. It was the exact same kind that her doctor had prescribed her.

Making a mental note, Carla would be sure to address Morgan, but it wouldn't be today. Carla headed back towards the stairs without a backwards glance, but if she had, she would have saw Morgan open her eyes and gently exhale.

CHAPTER 17

The Power of Prayer

E bony laid in bed next to a sleeping Ivan. Things were perfect, on the outside, but she felt like they were struggling with something so much deeper. After being served with court papers from Antoine, something had shifted. They still laughed, played and made love, but it felt guarded.

Both had agreed not to mention the custody battle to Amber until they were aware of the outcome. Yet, each day Ebony saw the light dim in Ivan's eyes and she knew exactly what he was feeling. There was a possibility that this man who had disappeared twelve years ago would come and claim a spot in Amber's life that Ivan and only Ivan had filled.

Ebony looked over at Ivan and her eyes filled with tears, she was scared. Scared that the outcome of tomorrow's hearing would shift her relationship, not just with her husband, but her daughter as well. She damned her life and the decisions that she had made. Realistically, she hadn't done anything wrong but birth a wonderful baby girl and marry an amazing man, but it all seemed like it was slowly crumbling at the hands of a former lover.

What really crushed Ebony's heart was the fact that they hadn't been able to have a child in the last eight years that they'd been trying. She looked at what Carla and Joshua had and she desired it. She wanted her husband to be present from the beginning through the end of her pregnancy; attending every doctor's appointment, comforting her while in pain and being a shoulder when she was sick. Even though Ivan had stepped in with Amber, Ebony had always felt guilty because he was taking care of someone else's responsibility.

Ebony knew she was overwhelmed with all of her thoughts, even though nothing was too hard for God. He was indeed the giver of life as well as the lawyer in the courtroom. Yet, in these two issues she hadn't turned them over to Him. She needed to increase her faith because she was seriously struggling in the Jesus department and it was starting to piss her off because she knew better.

Sliding out of the bed and onto her knees, Ebony did what her parents had taught her to do in difficult situations, she began to pray:

Lord I come to you, as humbly as I know how. Asking that you forgive me for my sins- knowing and unknowing. I ask that you touch my husband in a mighty special way oh God. Bless everything that his hands touch- every dream, every aspiration. I bind the spirit of negativity, insufficiencies, doubt and fear in the name of Jesus. I pray your choice blessings upon his life. Oh God make and mold him into the man that you'd want him to be. Tame his tongue, change his language, conform the worldly taste Oh God. I plead the blood of Jesus against illness, sickness, disease and generational curses that attach themselves to him.

I pray for an ear of clarity and discernment, that he leads this family as you would have. That he doesn't make a move without your leading. God I pray for his desire to work and provide, to create a level of stability, I come against

the mentality of addiction and poverty in the name of
Jesus. God, we thank you for everything that you've done
and everything that you're going to do. For your loving
kindness and the multitudes of your tender mercies.

God I also ask that you bless the fruit of his loins, for
healthy, mobile sperm in the name of Jesus. I know
that you are the giver of life and nothing is too hard for
you. God I place tomorrow's case in your hands, God
we ask that you bestow favor upon us. Be the judge and
Jury in the name of Jesus. And I bind anything from
hindering this prayer from reaching heaven in Jesus
Mighty Name. Signed, Sealed and Delivered. Amen.

Ebony rose the next morning feeling brand new. A
bubble of peace surrounded her and she refused to let anyone
disrupt that. After dropping Amber off at school, Ivan drove
towards the courthouse. Walking hand in hand, they met
Brandon at the assigned door. It was nice to have a lawyer
in the family. He was already privy to the knowledge and
history of her family, so they didn't have to plead their case
to him.

Everyone exchanged pleasantries: Ebony asked how
Morgan was and they moved on to the hearing that was
scheduled to take place in the next twenty minutes. The
closer the time drew, the more Ebony prayed that Antoine
wouldn't show at all and she could go back to her life as she
knew it.

Unfortunately, as the Bailiff called the court into
session and the Judge approached the bench, Antoine, his
mother and his lawyer also entered the court room. *Would*
the plaintiff like to present the case? She faintly heard the
judge ask.

Plaintiff: "Your honor, we're here in a child custody hearing because my client was recently informed that he fathered a child twelve years ago and the mother refuses to grant him access to see or speak with the child."

Defendant: "Your honor, my client is protecting the best interest of the child as the plaintiff has a record of inconsistency. The plaintiff has been absent the past twelve years that the child has been on this earth. The man who she currently calls dad, has stepped into his place."

Plaintiff: "Your honor, how was my client supposed to step in and help raise a child that he was not aware of?"

Defendant: "Your honor, he was not notified because he left my client a note when he disappeared and she hasn't seen or heard from him since."

Judge: "Okay, hold it. Mr. Taylor, please stand."

Antoine: "Yes, your honor."

Judge: "Amuse me. Certainly you have rights as a biological father, but give me a tangible explanation that prevents me from tying this case up in so many legalities that it takes two years before you're granted access to see your daughter. Give me a reason to disrupt the normalcy in Amber Johnson's life?"

Antoine: "Amber Johnson? Whose last name is that?"

Ebony rose and responded, "It's her father's name, the man that has raised and nurtured Amber since she took her first breath into this world. It's my husband's name."

Antoine: "I want her name changed."

Ebony: "You don't have that right or authority. Her name will not be changed, and it will reflect what it reflects now. Just as her birth certificate reflects him as the father. Your honor, he doesn't even live here, his residence is in another state. Will he pay child support for the last eleven years? Of course not, because he doesn't have a pot nor a window to piss in."

Judge: "Whoa, Mrs. Johnson, let's play a little nicer, shall we?"

Antoine: "I just want to see my daughter, get a chance to know her!"

Ebony had taken over as Brandon rested his case. "For how long? A week? A year? Two years? Your honor, my husband and I don't have a problem with him seeing his biological daughter. On the contrary, we do have a problem with his inconsistent behavior and the disruption and backlash that this will cause in our household. Antoine doesn't live there, he won't have to live with the hurt and disappointment of a little girl who feels like her parents lied and deceived her."

Judge: "Does the Plaintiff have a defense to the defendant?"

Plaintiff: "My client is not at liberty to make any commitments at this time because he is scheduled to return to work at the end of the week."

Judge: "So when will he be able to make a commitment? He's asking for custody of a child that he has never met, but he has to be back to work in another state, by the end of the week? Please help me understand how the child benefits here!"

Plaintiff: "May I have a moment to confer with my client?"

Judge: "Sure. Take two minutes, if you need them!"

Plaintiff: "Your honor, my client would like to take a recess to sort some things out."

Judge: "Sure, but it will not be today. We'll recess for ninety days. Mr. Taylor when you come back into my court room, you need to have some definitive answers for me.

Until then, Amber will remain in full custody with Mr. and Mrs. Johnson and it will be up to their discretion to allow you to see Amber."

Antoine leaned over to his lawyer, "Just another bitter black woman, we should have gotten a male Judge."

Judge: "Excuse you, young man? My job is to see to the best interest of the child not to an ego of an over sized little boy who ran instead of manning up to any responsibility that was left behind. I commend you Ivan Johnson for your remarkable character and unfaltering manhood. In fact, due to the immaturity and instability of the plaintiff, I will dismiss the case and surrender my notes accordingly. You will have to start the filing process from the beginning if you'd like to dispute my ruling. I will also be sure to notate the blatant disrespect shown by the plaintiff. Good day all."

Ebony turned towards Ivan who was seated right behind her and jumped into his arms. If Antoine wanted to meet Amber then he'd have to do it after she turned eighteen. By then, she'd be able to make her own decisions, but for now she only had one father, Ivan.

Walking into the hallway, Ebony hugged Brandon as she thanked him for his help. Even though, she barely allowed him to do his job. He promised to adjust her bill accordingly.

Coming face to face with Antoine, Ebony stepped into character mode as if she was in a western shoot'em up movie that her father loved to watch. She cocked her fingers as if it were a gun, fired it and blew the smoke off of the edge of her index finger. Just when Antoine thought she was finished, she mouthed the word *BITCH*, grabbed her husband's hand and walked out of the courthouse.

CHAPTER 18

Put Your Money Where Your Mouth Is!

*M*organ walked into her office and tried to get her mind right. It had been almost a week since she'd been back in the office and she only had fifteen minutes to prepare for her first client. Looking at the paperwork, she wasn't familiar with the name, so she assumed that she had a new client arriving. First impressions were always the most impressionable, she mumbled to herself.

When the knock came at the door, Morgan stood and waited for the client to enter, but she saw Carla instead. "Good Morning CeCe, but I have a new client on the way in." She explained.

"I am your client for today." Carla smiled.

"But the name I have here..." Morgan's voice trailed off to look at the schedule.

Carla waved her hand, "Just a little distraction so that you wouldn't have time to prepare for this meeting."

"Okay, do you need to talk more about Joshua?" Morgan inquired.

"No, Joshua and I are fine, thanks!"

"Okay so what's going on today?" Morgan left the pen and pad faced down.

"I was going to ask you the same question. Are you feeling better?"

"Yes I'm fine; I'm not sure what you mean." Morgan lied.

Carla hated when people played word games with her because she never did others like that. She tried to live by the code of *treating others the way she wanted to be treated.* If someone asked Carla a question, then she simply answered it. If people had the balls to let it roll off of their tongue then certainly she could honor it with an honest answer.

"Okay let's try another approach." Carla stared at the muted Morgan. "Are you pregnant?"

Morgan shifted. "What are you getting at?"

"I simply asked you a question. I came in here like the rest of your clients, spilled my guts and personal affairs and solidified it with a confidential clause and you say, *Should you be offended that I hadn't come to you as a friend.* But you've been walking around as if everything's okay." Carla spat.

"I believe that everyone is entitled to their own business." Morgan confessed.

"Oh, your pregnancy is your business, but mine was everyone's business. I, for sure remember you giving your opinion about me aborting my baby because I didn't really know the father and I'd be a single parent, blah, blah, blah." Carla mocked.

"And yet here you are, ready to pop. So what's your point?" Morgan's patience was beginning to thin.

"My point is that, I've been there for every aspect of your life. In your darkest moments and some of your proudest, I've been there. When you got married and when Skylar was born." Carla pointed at her chest. "I believe I was there. Every pep talk, every counseling session where you couldn't counsel yourself, I was there. For every insane scenario that required an insane accomplice rather than rationality, it was me, I was there.. Then you had the balls not to show your face, not one time during my baby shower!"

"I let you use my house for God's sake, what more did you want from me?" Morgan yelled.

"Would you like a cookie for that? You volunteered your house; we didn't ask you for it." Carla reminded.

Morgan was tired of the bullshit and she didn't have time to sit and let Carla bust her balls all morning, so she caved. "I'm pregnant, but we're not sure for how much longer. The doctor's believe that I am threatening a miscarriage because I have lupus. So excuse me if I couldn't be your cheerleader because I had my own fucking problems to deal with. Maybe, just maybe, I didn't want to watch your pregnant ass wobbling across the yard, opening gifts and having a merry good time. Maybe my feelings are hurt that Skylar may be my last child and it's possible that I am unable to be happy for you and be a friend in this hour. For once, you'll have to do something on your own."

Morgan stood and straightened her clothes. "So if you're done with this *Shake down.*" Morgan used her fingers to show the quotations. "Then this session will be voided and recorded as charity and consider yourself dismissed."

Carla stood to her feet, but not before acknowledging several statements. "I'm not a foreigner when it comes to miscarriages; I'm very familiar with being around people with babies while your heart is breaking for your own. But, somehow I've always managed to be there for you and to be your cheerleader. But, I'll leave you to your business as I have my own to attend to." When Carla reached the door, she called out over her shoulder, "Good luck with the lupus,

God is even bigger than that." Carla opened the door and shut it quietly behind her.

****

Joshua watched as Carla ran the vacuum, washed the dishes, dusted the television and set the table. Her mind was racing and he could tell. He heard the hurt and disappointment in her voice when she called him at work during the earlier part of the week, regarding Morgan. He figured that by the time he'd made it down for the weekend that they would have made up. From the look of things, he was incorrect. It had been two weeks since the baby shower, which put Carla at thirty four weeks and Joshua was worried about her blood pressure.

Coming up behind her, he put his arms around her. "It's going to be okay baby, I'm right here and you've got a whole support system behind you. You're going to have a helleva handsome son that's going to look just like his daddy. Everything's been prepared for him to come whenever he gets ready." Carla encircled his arms around her. "Don't worry about anything else; what's meant to be will be." Joshua kissed the crown of Carla's head.

It was rare that Joshua lost his cool about anything, so it was easy for him to tell Carla not to worry. He was an only child, he didn't have many friends, at least not ones that he trusted and he didn't have a big family. Joshua didn't understand how Carla felt, but she appreciated his comfort and reassurance that he offered. Something had shifted in a twenty year friendship and she was slowly trying to come to terms with that. Carla felt as if she had experienced a bad break up and a small void had been left. For the first couple of days she couldn't stop the tears from falling, but by the end of the week, she was just numb. There were just certain behaviors that she expected from certain people, and the level of disappointment that she felt was astounding. Although, the sound truth was that the only person who owed her anything was Joshua. Her sisters nor her friends, owed her anything and if they did something, it was considered an addition.

Instead of trying to express those feelings to Joshua, Carla simply went back to preparing for the arrival of her guests for the *couples* game night. Ebony was bringing Ivan, of course, and Carla had invited James to be Chrissey's date. There were some sure sparks there, but Carla wouldn't interfere anymore than she already had. She'd simply sit back and observe.

******

Grabbing her glass of wine, Chrissey sat next to James. "Okay, so I have a topic for discussion."

Before she could finish, Carla mumbled, "Dear God." She made eye contact with Ebony, pleading with her eyes for some interference.

Ebony caught the familiar glance and decided to help, "Bring it!" She shouted, knowing that was the only encouragement Chrissey needed to get started. Meanwhile Carla reached behind her and threw the decorative pillow at Ebony. Unfortunately, Ebony caught it. Ebony had run track in high school and participated in shot put. The sport was designed to throw heavy things. She was a jack of all trades; there wasn't anything that she couldn't do.

Chrissey snapped her fingers, gathering everyone's attention. "Ok, here we go. What's the price of coochie?"

Carla simply put her face in the palm of her hands, she was mortified! Chrissey was so embarrassing. She looked at a laughing Joshua as he encircled his arm around her protruding waist, or what used to be a waist.

Chrissey sobered from laughing at the expressions on everyone's face. "No, listen I'm so serious, let's talk about this." She turned towards James and said, "How much do you think my nana is worth?"

James moved from his spot on the couch, "I think I need another drink for this shit here."

"No, don't run." Chrissey called after him. "Listen, let's do the math." Yelling in James' direction, "I need a number dammit, how much?"

James came back and sat next to Chrissey as he rubbed his hand over his goatee. "For starters, let's just say it's worth $500,000 right?" James waited until Chrissey nodded. "But, then you gotta think about how many men you've slept with and then start subtracting $10,000 for each man, I mean it really depends on how much they stretched the coochie."

Joshua laughed again. He was more amused at the look on Chrissey's face rather than the insult itself.

"Ok, that's fine." Chrissey pulled out her calculator. "So we subtract $60,000. from my total that leaves me with $440,000."

"True, but then we have to subtract the age, so for every year that you've had sex, since you've become sexually active, subtract another $5,000…"

When Chrissey heard Ivan snicker, she looked at Joshua and said, "I guess that's why old men date younger women."

This time, Carla laughed and Joshua responded and said, "You's a dirty mothafucker. You just keep subtracting over there, cause I know you've been fucking for a long time." The room ruptured in laughter and Chrissey wasn't offended at all.

"You damn right, I taught your girl everything she knows. That's why yo ass sitting here right now, cause you got caught up in the sauce, boo." Chrissey turned and winked at Carla. "It's a Williams' thing. And umm, you're welcome mothafucka."

Mocking a stance of royalty, Joshua stood and bowed at the waist. "We sure do appreciate you and all your training, your highness. Although, there were a few things that I had to perfect - you didn't quite teach them without flaw, but from a woman's stance, you did alright."

Ivan opened his mouth to chime in, but Ebony put her hand over it to close it.

"Oh no, let that man speak." Joshua was more vocal than normal because this was his domain. He was always more relaxed when he could control the environment. "It's okay bro, there was some shit you had to tweak too, huh?"

Chrissey picked up a pillow and tossed it in Joshua's direction. "Fuck you cornbread."

"Aww don't be mad sis, you can act like a man all you want and you can be as hard as you want, but you'll always be a woman. You're just as soft as your sisters." He smirked. "But I ain't gonna lie, you know a little bit about the game, I peeped you!"

Chrissey's only reply was her middle finger because she couldn't deny his observation. She liked Joshua for several reasons. The main reason was because he was honest and another was because he loved her sister. All the other bullshit in between didn't concern her. Love was an awkward emotion. It made people do the unthinkable, say the unbelievable, and observe the irrefutable, but it bordered between genuine love and lust.

Speaking of lust, Chrissey's attention shifted to James who was seated next to her and she wondered what it would be like to be underneath him. To have his arms holding her still while he climbed her body and slid his powerful penis between her thighs. She licked her lips in anticipation. She knew it was inevitable; the chemistry was slowly wearing her down. Soon he'd find out just how much her coochie was really worth and numbers wouldn't do it justice.

Out of the corner of her eye, Chrissey noticed the discomfort on Carla's face, "You okay, sis?"

Carla shifted on the sofa. "Yes, I just need to pee." When she lifted off of the sofa with Joshua's help, she felt the trickle of liquid begin to release. "Oh no, I think I peed on myself." Joshua ran his hand down her legs and Carla's teary eyes stared into his as he smelled the wetness on his fingers. "No baby, that's your water. Your water broke."

Carla wasn't sure whether to be happy or sad, she still had three more weeks before she was considered full term. She needed to keep the baby inside as long as possible.

Ebony, who was used to taking charge, shifted into action. "Okay, its ok. Have you packed the baby's bag?"

Running upstairs and gathering everything necessary, Ebony stuffed items into the designer Gucci diaper bag that Chrissey had purchased for Baby JJ. Loading the cars, everyone sped in the direction of Providence Hospital when Carla called to say that she had chosen Henry Ford West Bloomfield. She could imagine her sisters cussing the whole time, considering the hospital was twenty minutes in the opposite direction.

Dropping Carla off at the Emergency door, Joshua went to park the car while her sisters assisted her inside of the state of the art facility. Chrissey was the first one to approach the front desk when the receptionist told her that Carla would have to wait to be seen.

Chrissey stood back, appalled. "You don't see her coochie juices spilling all over the place? In a minute I'm going to have to call Noah and ask him to bring his ark, just to save us." Ebony snickered, Chrissey was a fool. "You've got forty-five seconds to get her doctor before I become a disturbance in this beautiful place of healing." Chrissey turned and rubbed Carla's forehead "You okay, Pooh Pooh?" From observation, one would determine that Chrissey sometimes babied Carla. It was the motherly instinct in her that she often tried to suppress. Chrissey held the wolf pack territorial claim because she didn't play about her sister, either one of them.

It wasn't a secret that Chrissey and Carla had a special bond, mainly because they were a little closer in age, but also because Carla hurt herself at fourteen years old. It caused Chrissey to take care of Carla while she learned to walk again after several surgeries. The incident occurred in gym class, but the tearing of the ligaments in her knee and the destruction of the nerves in her foot caused more damage than the natural eye could estimate.

Ebony laughed at how bi-polar Chrissey could be, she had gone from calm to crazy on the receptionist in three point three seconds, flat. Needless to say it took more than forty-five seconds for them to tend to Carla's condition, but certainly less than twenty minutes.

After careful examination, Carla hadn't started dilating but they weren't able to send her home because she'd lost some of her amniotic fluid. The doctor wanted to monitor the baby to make sure that he was able to survive inside of Carla's womb as long as possible before forcing his way into the world.

Chrissey came into the room and plopped down in one chair and Ebony took the other. That left Joshua, James and Ivan standing. Since Joshua wasn't going anywhere anytime soon, he copped a squat on Carla's bed, dropping his arm around her stomach. "How are you feeling, Baby?"

"I'm okay!"

"You sure? You worried?" Joshua skeptically questioned.

Shaking her head, she admitted, "God's got him, I believe that." She caressed his cheek. "There's no need for us to worry. He's healthy and he's going to be just fine." Looking over at the heart monitor, Carla watched the lines go up and down, confirming that her son was indeed alive and well.

"Did anybody call Mommy and Daddy?" Carla interrupted her sister's side bar conversation. Their look of cluelessness verified that they hadn't. "Well, can someone call them?"

Joshua spoke up before Ebony could take her cell phone out of her purse. "I already called your father, Babe!" He placed his index finger under Carla's chin to close her mouth that seemed to have parted at the revelation.

Chrissey was the first one to break the silence. "Oh, well look at the balls on that man. That's what I'm talking about, take control of the situation. This is your baby, show daddy who's wearing the big draws."

It didn't take a rocket scientist to know there was tension between Carlos and Joshua. Chrissey and Ebony just made it their business to mind their own business. Daddies were always going to be daddies no matter how old their children were. He was the father, the priest of his house and until all of his daughters were married, he'd remain in his position.

Stopping Carla from asking the question that was lodged in her throat, the nurse entered the room. Joshua slid to the bottom of the bed, thinking that the space should suffice until the nurse announced that she would like to check Carla's cervix again since an hour had passed. Only Ivan and James moved.

When Joshua eyed Ebony and Chrissey, Chrissey was sure to notify him of her position. "That Coochie ain't people shy. I'm not leaving. I don't want second hand information; I want to hear it straight from the horse's mouth.

Joshua nodded and Ebony chorused. "Neigh."

Carla laughed as she remembered the conversation that she and her sisters had several weeks ago. "For your information, my coochie has seen less people than your $395,000 coochie. I'm still at $435,000."

"That's because you didn't calculate them one night stands." Carla choked as Chrissey continued to come for her. "Oh freaky, kinky ass." Turning towards the awaiting nurse, Chrissey addressed her, "Ms. Nurse Ma'am, please proceed and check her, my nephew is waiting."

Carla wasn't going to argue with her, it was no use, so she laid back and spread her legs.

With gentle precision, the nurse diagnosed. "Ok, it looks like you're at one. He probably won't be born until tomorrow morning. In most cases, moms can stay between one and two centimeters for hours and sometimes, days."

Carla watched Ebony and Chrissey look at each other and immediately she knew they were trying to leave her.

Noticing the fear in her eyes, Joshua leaned over and whispered so only she could hear him. "I love you and I'm right here with you. I know that you love them, but they have their own families to tend too. I promise to keep them updated with any changes for you." Giving her hand a gentle squeeze, Carla looked into Joshua's eyes and nodded that she agreed and understood. "You, Him and I are a family and I always take care of my family." Joshua kissed away the tears that she let fall.

"It's probably too late to warn my parents so they'll have to just find out once they get here." Carla said to no one in particular.

In unison, Ebony and Chrissey promised, "We'll come back first thing in the morning!"

Joshua promised back, "I'll call you guys if he threatens to come sooner."

Chrissey walked into the hallway and bumped into James, gently grabbing the front of his button up shirt. "Follow me home?"

James raised his eyebrows to confirm his understanding and Chrissey stepped closer to verify that he comprehended correctly. She could have suggested his place, but she thought better of it.

Men were liars and women were nuts. Chrissey knew no one had a key to her house except her. She wasn't sure if the same went for James. She didn't know who he was involved with and she didn't care. Chrissey had one goal in mind and her kitty kat was in total agreement.

Sliding the key in the back door, Chrissey looked over her shoulder at James. "There's no going back once you cross this threshold."

"What's understood doesn't need to be explained." He countered her response.

"And there will be no mercy, bloody Mary, or crying for your mama either!"

"I'm a big boy, I can handle it!" James confirmed for her once again.

Chrissey turned around and completely pressed her breast against his, slipping her hand in between his legs, she whispered, "Just how big of a boy are you?"

"Big enough to take you to heaven, stop for food and water and then bring you back, while shattering you to pieces."

"We'll see!" That was the last thing either of them said as they entered Chrissey's condo through the garage. "Do you need a shower?" She didn't want no funky dick just as much as he didn't want a funky coochie.

James shrugged out of his jacket and laid it over a chair before responding. "Only if you join me!"

Smiling at the offer, Chrissey walked into the bathroom and manipulated the handles for a nice, steamy atmosphere. Undressing and signaling for him to come near, Chrissey turned her back and walked towards the shower stall. Once inside, James pinned her to the wall before she could turn around.

The weight of his erection hung in between the cheeks of her rear as he clutched both of her arms and arrested them against the wall above her head. He whispered in her ear, "Does he feel big enough for you?"

She moaned instead of responding and he slapped his length against her. There was something about being blinded by such a magnificent surprise. The anticipation alone was eating her alive. All she needed to do was get her mouth around the head and he was hers. When Chrissey tried to wiggle free, he turned her around, but he didn't release her. Before she could protest or challenge him, he cut off her will power with the blunt force trauma of his lips. They were the softest, most plush, gentle pair of pleasure that she'd ever encountered. Her inner freak sagged and the moisture between her thighs increased.

James inclined his body into Chrissey, giving into the pleasure that he was sure he'd find. The part of his brain that said you can't have sex in the shower because you don't have a condom was cut off when Chrissey began climbing his body. He freed her hands to use the wall as his balance as he positioned his penis in between her thighs and at the apex of her opening. Knowing what she craved, he gripped both of her legs, encircled them around his waist and invaded her body. It was the gasp that broke the kiss and the rising pleasure that made her brain scramble.

If anyone ever said that length and width didn't matter, they were liars from the pit of hell. But, Chrissey couldn't afford to be dazed, she had a point to prove and a representation to uphold. Gyrating her hips and coercing her body to accommodate him, caused him to falter.

The deeper he stroked, the harder he fell. He'd witnessed first hand what kryptonite was like. The more he plunged, the more she gushed with juices. Her muscles seemed to be working overtime as they contracted to hold him hostage inside of her. "Witch." He whispered.

"You might as well go ahead and cum, I know you want too!" Chrissey taunted.

"I won't come before you, I can do this all night baby." To add emphasis to his point, he placed his hands underneath her hips and drove deeper, longer and harder. It wasn't until Chrissey began pounding her fist onto his chest that he realized that she was close. He thought he had won the verbal spat until her vaginal muscles gripped him with a force that froze his body and made him loosen his hold on her. If his reflexes had been any slower, she would have slid down the shower wall. The rush that lifted from his sack and traveled through his shaft at the abrupt impulse caused his release to begin where Chrissey's had ended.

James wanted to move, he needed to pull out of her, but he was glued. It was the ringing of Chrissey's cell phone that shattered the moment of sensation.

"It could be Joshua calling." Chrissey's voice was heavy with weariness.

"Well, you better hurry and wash off!"

When Chrissey reached for her phone, the phone call was followed by a text message. The interruption was Ebony and not Joshua:

> *You ain't nothing but a squirrel, you*
> *just had to have that nut!*

Chrissey laughed while replying

> *And what was a wonderful nut it was.*
> *Klink Klink*

Sneaking up behind her, James stood with a towel wrapped around his waist. "Is Chrissey okay?"

"It was Ebony. But, I did text Joshua to check on Carla!" Chrissey dropped her phone as she spun around.

"Okay." Nodding his head up and down, he stuck his lip out as if there was more that he wanted to say.

"You good?" She inquired.

"Oh yeah, you?"

"Of course. You were good." She smiled. "Much better than I expected."

"What were you expecting?" James moved in closer.

"I mean, I expected you to be good."

"But…" James was waiting for the punch line.

Chrissey wanted to tell him that round two would help her determine the *but*, but instead she said, "But, now I need to calculate how much your dick is worth, how many miles is on it and how long you've been fucking." Chrissey was a thug, she didn't fall in love with dick and she had no intentions of starting today. But her inner freak was certainly doing the happy dance, she'd found a keeper. Chrissey had a secret gift of spotting good dick anyway, but there was something special about James.

"Umph." James pulled Chrissey into his embrace. "So, do you have a rule about letting men spend the night?" He changed the subject.

"Of course I do."

"What is it?" He inquired, but held his breath as a precaution.

"The first time is free, but the second time, you have to contribute to a bill." Chrissey informed.

"What?" James asked baffled.

"What do you mean, what? First of all, coochie is not free." Chrissey started in on him, "And neither is my light and gas bill. The first time is a courtesy; the second time is a charge." She smiled sweetly.

James let her go and went in search of his pants. The first thing Chrissey thought was that she'd ran into another cheap ass negro who thought it was free to drink from the cow rather than purchase it. Instead, he reached into his pants pocket and peeled off a one hundred dollar bill and set it on her dresser. "It was an honor being in your presence tonight, the money is for the dinner that I should have treated you too."

"Well…" She paused, silently taken back by the action. "If that is for dinner, then I need you to add another hundred next to it. I normally eat crab legs at dinner and they're two hundred dollars, a meal." Chrissey crossed her arms over her chest, refusing to smile.

Doing as she instructed, James set another hundred dollar bill on the dresser and said, "If I can foot the bill for dinner, then you're certainly going to work your ass off for dessert."

Chrissey was silent as James unwrapped the towel from around his waist. Genuinely smiling for the first time in weeks, Chrissey was going to enjoy tonight because tomorrow would change the game plan, indefinitely.

CHAPTER 19

The Element of Surprise!

*A*fter eighteen hours of active labor, he was finally here. Gorgeous with a head full of finely crafted hair that definitely came from Joshua's mixed ancestry. The baby was darker than Carla expected, she was almost certain that he was going to come out nice and pink. From the complexion of his ears, baby Joshua would be every bit of brown sugar. His chubby cheeks and pudgy nose was absolutely Carla's. It was the only hereditary trait that she contributed to the conception of her perfect son.

Picking him up out of the bassinet, Joshua cooed, "Look at Daddy's little man." Kissing his rather plum cheeks and cradling his son to his chest, Joshua peeked at Carla. "You look super sleepy, Mama."

Carla smiled at her new name, *Mama*. "I am, but I feel like if I close my eyes he might disappear. Like maybe this is a dream and I conjured you two up."

Joshua put the baby back in the bassinet near the hospital bed as he moved over to cradle Carla as he had previously done his son. "Naw Mama, it's real. Maybe a little too real. Yet, real nonetheless."

She looked at him with tear-filled eyes as she lifted her hand to caress his cheek, she whispered, "I Love You!"

"Certainly not as much as I've come to love you. I believe that they call people like you, *Blessings in Disguise.*"

She wouldn't disagree with that.

Rising from the bed, Joshua began looking for his car keys. "I'm going to the house to take a shower, change my clothes, grab something to eat and come back."

"How long will that take?" Carla questioned.

"No more than two hours. I'll be back before you know it. What do you want to eat, Chinese?"

She could only smile, he knew her so well! "Oh and you wonder why I love you. The quickest way to my heart is through my stomach."

"I thought that saying was only reserved for men?"

"Well, I am a woMAN and a feMALE, so it's befitting." Carla assured.

Joshua cocked his head to stare at Carla sideways, "I'mma need you to spread your legs again, let me recheck the merchandise. I'd hate to think I was being bamboozled."

Carla grabbed at his penis. "Ask *him*. He'll confirm all that you need to know."

"You think *he* knows you better than I do?" Joshua asked.

"I think that he's your eyes in places that you can't see." She winked.

"After today, I think I've seen all there is to see." Joshua shivered at the thought of labor.

"Was it that bad?" Carla laughed while crossing her legs.

"Let's just say, I'd rather not have to see it again."

"This is your fifth child, you should be a pro." Carla laughed.

Joshua corrected, "Fifth Child, first delivery."

Carla was going to inquire further, but decided against it. She was just grateful that he had been there with her. "Duly noted." Carla blew a kiss at him. "Two hours or I'm calling the State Troopers, Fire Marshalls as well as the Army Reserve to come and find your hind parts."

"Two Hours." He promised as he leaned over and kissed her goodbye.

It appeared that as soon as Carla's head hit the pillow, she drifted off to sleep. Shortly after, there was a cool draft that swept over her that quickly woke her. Sure enough the presence of her ex- husband had manifested. "Please put him down, Dre."

"Shh, I'm not going to hurt him." Dre gently rubbed the baby's hair.

Carla wasn't sure if he'd hurt her son or not, but she wasn't one for taking chances. She reached for the nurse's button when she heard the baby whine.

Dre peeped her game and shifted the baby from one arm to the other. "That won't be necessary Carla, I just wanted to see you." He jerked his shoulder. "Check on you." Dre walked over to the chair that Joshua had vacated. "I see he was able to give you what I couldn't."

"I'd feel a lot better about this conversation, if you put the baby down, Dre." She reiterated.

Raising his voice a bit, Dre showed his aggravation. "Didn't I say that I wouldn't hurt him?"

"You're the last person whose word is something that I trust."

"Oh it's just as bankable as your Alimony checks."

"It pays to play, doesn't it? Or in your case, it really pays." Carla giggled.

"The way I see it, technically, he's my son too. I mean I am taking care of him!"

"Wrong again dummy. You take care of me and I take care of him. You want some responsibility to take care of?

Then please go and grab you a hoe or two. I'm sure there is more where Jasmine came from?"

"That's a low blow." Dre squirmed a bit.

"Well I tried to play nice, but you're still holding my son after I asked you to put him down, twice." Carla wiggled two of her fingers.

Dre ignored her as he looked down into the sleeping baby's face. "I really wanted to give you this. I wanted to be a good husband and a great father."

Slightly interested, Carla asked, "So why weren't you?"

"Monkey- see, Monkey- do."

"Pardon me?"

"In my line of work, it's all a game. Who can get to the top the quickest and who can manipulate the system the fastest!"

"Okay…" Carla nodded as she tried to process exactly what the hell Dre was talking about.

"Women." He said forcefully, startling the baby. "Women are the key manipulators in any game that is played with a room full of men. Married or unmarried, all men have a price."

"Weak men have a price." Carla spat. Dre remained silent, so Carla continued, "What was your price?"

"You. I paid the ultimate price." He whispered. "Greed cost me, you!"

"So greed made you cheat?" Carla smacked her lips and was tempted to roll her eyes.

"I had to play the game if I wanted to win at being the best, at obtaining the most. Dammit I had to become invincible, untouchable. I never wanted us to struggle and I never wanted us to starve, but I sacrificed the sanctity of our marriage for a rendezvous with the master of manipulation."

Nodding her head slowly, Carla was trying to process it all. "So the bet?" Carla asked for the first time since she became aware of the deception her ex- husband and Joshua had conjured.

Dre leaned his head to the side and smirked. "The bet was a desperate act to try and persuade you to come back to me. It was a childish game and I believe that losing you a second time hurt more than the first."

"I don't want to come back, Dre!"

"I know and I've accepted that." He pouted. "Promise me one thing…"

Carla cocked her head. "What?"

"That if you ever need anything that you'll let me be the one to see to your needs."

"Why? Do you plan on making Joshua a casualty?"

"Of course not, but every dog has its day and I'm in your corner if the day comes sooner than later."

"Is that right?" Carla silently questioned if this was more of his mind games. She quietly watched Dre kiss the crown of her sons head and place him back in the bassinet. She'd unconsciously released the anxiety that she held since she'd awaken. A peace consumed her as Dre kissed her cheek and whispered, "That's right."

She still loved him, she always would, just not in the capacity that he wanted her too. Their days were done. She'd lived and she'd loved and she'd learned and now she had someone to love her back.

Rocking her son in her arms, she started praying over him. She didn't know what kind of baby-bubblegum- bullshit Dre had rubbed off on her son, but today was not the day, Satan.

The more she looked at her son, the more she wondered where her sisters were.

****

Chrissey sat in a room with double glass and she gladly gave it the middle finger. She wanted whoever was on the other side of the window to know that they could kiss her natural born ass. She had things to do and places to go.

When the door finally opened, James walked through it.

"Oh thank God." Chrissey breathed. "Will you get me out of here? This is crazy, this can't be about some funky ass license." Chrissey was pulled over by the police with the allegation that she was speeding, but she hadn't been, at least not today.

"You're right, its not, we gotta talk. How many times do I have to tell you to pay your tickets and get your license fixed?"

"Yeah, but I didn't think you were serious." Chrissey rolled her eyes as if to say, duh! "Okay so let's talk business, what's going on?"

"Everything isn't as it seems." James fidgeted in his chair a bit.

"No shit, as far as what?" Chrissey interrogated.

Before James could answer, the door opened again and Daniel walked inside. "Such as this." James added. "I'd like you to meet undercover Agent Ryan Daniels."

"Who the fuck is Ryan Daniels? I thought his name was Daniel Beasley." Chrissey folded her arms and sat back in the chair.

"No, that's his undercover name." James confirmed.

Chrissey looked Daniel up and down. "So my boyfriend wasn't really my boyfriend?" Chrissey wasn't asking anyone in particular, but it started to piss her off when no one said anything. "So are you gonna say something or you just gonna keep staring at me, Daniel? Ryan? Undercover Agent Man?"

"What do you want me to say other than you owe me a new car." Daniel crossed his arms over his chest.

"You're the big agent boo, charge that shit to the game." Chrissey flicked him off and turned her attention back to James. "So what's this all about?"

"Daniel took down a team of suppliers yesterday and they're looking for him. They think it was simply a hit, but nonetheless, you may be next on the list once they can't find him."

"So not only did you two assholes take out a team and possibly put us all in danger, you're also counterfeits?" Chrissey asked.

"No one messed up, that's why we're taking this precaution. And there are no counterfeits here, he's an undercover agent and I was covering his back." James explained.

"And the part where you screwed me was what?" Chrissey grilled him.

"Enjoyable to say the least." James complimented while letting his eyes soften.

"Wait, you fucked my girl, dawg?" Daniel got up from the table.

"Naw Baby, he made sweet leisurely love to me. And since when am I your girl? You tried to fucking kill me."

"I was trying to protect you, things were getting difficult and someone was turning up the heat. If I could prove that you and I were at odds, then you would be of no use to them." Daniel explained.

"And the girl?" Chrissey questioned further.

"What girl?" Daniel questioned.

"The girl from the hotel?"

"She was a CI!" Daniel explained further when Chrissey gave him a blank stare. "A criminal informant."

"This is all bullshit. Fake ass wanna be boyfriend and gang banger." Chrissey was starting to lose her cool. One, because she misjudged the situation and two, because she felt like they played her. "Then you got this chivalry counterfeit mother fucker going along with the shit, stalking me and adding to the mind games."

"First off, I wasn't playing mind games and if anyone is a counterfeit, it's you and your sisters. You go around pretending to be things that you aren't when you're nothing more than church girls and preacher's kids." James had taken the time to analyze them, observe their behaviors, dissect it and then make a final assessment.

"Oh spare me dick breath." Chrissey insulted. "I don't need you to read me my biblical rights. Either you assholes are going to charge me with something or you're going to let me go. I was in the midst of heading somewhere when you stopped me."

"You and that mouth." James warned.

"You should have put a muzzle on that shit." Daniel directed his comment towards James.

"Tell Carla congrats on the baby." James suddenly realized where Chrissey might have been headed too.

"I ain't telling her shit, tell her yourself liar liar." Chrissey was still fuming.

"I didn't lie!"

"Yada Yada." She threw her hand at him as a dismissal.

"Are you two finished yet?" Daniel interrupted.

"There's nothing counterfeit or pretentious about me?" Chrissey argued.

"Oh, so you know other words besides Gucci and Fendi." Daniel insulted.

"Yeah bitch like, *Yo Mama*." Chrissey got out of her chair and was just around the table to get in his ass when James stopped her. She didn't give one shit about laws or rules, regulations or protocols, she was going for blood.

"Whoa ok, time out." James interrupted. "Both of you, go to separate corners."

"If you aren't careful we'll keep your big head ass here for a week." Daniel threatened.

James interjected before Chrissey could respond. "Twenty-four hours, that's all I'm asking. We just want to make sure that you're safe. You'll probably have to move from your condo, change up your normal patterns and rearrange your schedule, but you'll be safe." James was soft on her, he had gotten to know her and he liked what he saw on the surface and underneath.

"I'm not moving from my condo." Chrissey would do anything except that. Finally calm enough to understand the weight of the situation, Chrissey was defeated and exhausted. "At least let me call my parents. My sister was expecting me at the hospital."

James pulled Chrissey's chair out and gestured towards the door for her to make her call in private. Daniel opened the door, watching Chrissey as she exited. When Daniel came face to face with James, he lowered his voice and said, "You know this wont work, don't you?"

"She's smart, but we're smarter. Keep your head in the game, we're at the home stretch." James chastised.

Daniel tried to shake the eerie feeling that he was having. "You think you know her, but she's worse than Zoe Saldana in Columbiana. You better watch her little light skinned ass."

Chrissey made calls to her parents and her sisters, informing them that she'd be out of touch for the next 24 hours. She listened to Carla whine and Ebony fuss, but nothing compared to the hysterical animations of her mother who demanded more of an explanation.

When Chrissey approached the open door, she looked at the two idiots that had gotten her into this mess and asked, "So are you going to feed me or are you two fruit cakes going to continue staring into each others eyes like love sick puppies?"

James cleared his throat to find an appropriate response to her remark, but found none. "I'm going to show you to the holding cell and then I'll get you some food."

Chrissey felt her body respond in a convulsive manner as she geared to snatch somebody's ass. "If you think you're going to treat me like a regular inmate, then you've got the game fucked up. If you want my cooperation, then you can advise me of the location of your residence."

"Where I reside?" James asked confused.

"Yes the structure where you lay your head. I need the address and a spare key." Chrissey clarified for James.

James looked at Daniel who had put his head down to hide his amusement. For the first time since the operation began, James may have miscalculated the stakes. If he wanted Chrissey, then he'd have to play by her rules.

Hesitantly, placing the keys in Chrissey's awaiting palm, James silently cursed.

Chrissey smiled and inwardly did a happy dance, she checked the time on her custom Pearl Diamond Rolex Datejust watch and mumbled, "Show Time…"

CHAPTER 20

To Know Them - Is To Love Them!!!

*E*bony sat on the sofa in Chrissey's living room, surrounded by her sisters. She had some news that she wanted to share with them, but she would wait for the best timing. Right now, everyone's attention was glued to baby Joshua.

"Aww, give me my baby." Chrissey lifted the baby out of Carla's arms. She was never one to really ask for things, she just kind of assumed she had the authority to *take* what she wanted.

"Your baby?" Ebony questioned. "I thought Amber was your baby?"

Chrissey smirked, somebody was jealous. "Yeah she was, ten years ago. Don't nobody want that grown ass girl." Chrissey laughed when Ebony's face fell to the floor. "Just last week, she was asking what her limit for her Christmas list was."

"Well you give nice gifts, what did you expect from her?" Ebony came to her daughter's defense.

"I expected her ten year old ass…"

"She's eleven." Ebony cut Chrissey off.

"Well that's even worse. I expected her eleven year old ass to ask for simple things like – a doll house or an easy bake oven, not a Louis Vuitton wristlet and the matching shoes."

Carla laughed and joined the conversation for the first time. "That's what you get for spoiling her like that for the last ten years." Carla lifted her hand as she listed the countless items. "Burberry Shirts, Coach Belts, Hunter Boots, those one karat earrings and the matching charm bracelet. Surely you knew that you were forming a habit and creating a level of expectation."

Ebony laughed because Carla had a point and Chrissey had no way of denying it.

"That's fine. But Louie is on another level and I'll buy it for her, but not until she turns sixteen and not a day before that." Chrissey stated as a matter of fact and turned her back to rock the baby in her arms.

"And I don't know why you're laughing Ebony, because she has more apple electronics than a repair shop." Carla turned on Ebony next.

Ebony raised her hand to defend herself. "Oh give me a break Carla, you sound just like mommy. *If you give that girl everything at a young age then what will she have to look forward to when she's older?*"

"Mommy is such a hard ass." Chrissey agreed.

"Um don't come for her, neither one of you heathens." Carla reprimanded. "She should have been harder on you, Chrissey. I don't know what twenty six year old has been to jail more times than you." Carla insulted before turning to Ebony. "And if you'd listen to mommy, Ebony, then Amber wouldn't be turning into a miniature Nicki Minaj with taste buds of a Kardashian."

Chrissey was the first one to go in, "First of all Bitch…" Chrissey paused for emphasis, "You and I both know that the first two times were not my fault."

"No?" Carla asked in denial.

"No they weren't, so let the sleeping dogs, lie." Chrissey rolled her eyes.

Carla put her head down to cover her amusement. "Ok, so let's talk about this time. How'd you get arrested the other day and where have your light skinned tail been."

Chrissey took a deep breath and began, "Thatpunkasssonofabitchtriedtoplaymeafterifuckedhis brainsoutandmadehimcallhismama."

Ebony put her hands up to silence Chrissey. "What the hell did you just say?"

Chrisseyrolledhereyes."Isaid,thatpunkasssonofabitch..."

Carla bust out laughing. "Time out, time out. Which one?"

"Wait, you understood that mess?" Ebony asked confused. Chrissey was speaking so fast that it seemed as if there were no spaces between her words, which made it hard for Ebony to keep up.

"Yes sister, tap into your inner ghetto." Carla laughed some more. "Go ahead and continue Chrissey."

"DanielandJamestriedtoplayusalltheyarenotwhothey saidtheywereandihopethesonsofbitchesburninhell."

Ebony turned to Carla. "So you understood that too, huh?"

"Of course I did." Carla wiggled her nose.

"Then translate it for me." Ebony coerced.

"The short version of the dilemma is that her slut ass slept with both of them and they double crossed her."

Chrissey flicked Carla the middle finger in her defense.

Carla shook her head; she knew Chrissey was bout to go in on her when she increased her rocking speed with the baby. "Wait before you go in on me, do you have some clean towels?"

"Clean towels for what?"

"I want to freshen up. Hello? I just had a baby!"

"Oh hell naw, you got blood in your panties?" Chrissey cringed.

"Just a little!" Carla smacked.

"Well I don't have no towels for that, I only have white towels."

"Well what about the towels that you use for your cycle?" Ebony asked.

"I get a period once a year, who needs those?" Chrissey informed.

"That's probably why your ass always so angry, your hormones are all the way off." Ebony concluded.

Chrissey flicked her *the finger*.

Carla ignored them and walked towards the linen closet while Chrissey yelled after her, "When you're done, you throw that bitch in the garbage before you leave."

"Whatever." Carla threw over her shoulder.

"And I mean the garbage outside." Chrissey was too irritated. "Nasty Hoe."

Ebony laughed at her sister, Chrissey was a complete fool. "Umm, can you turn the heat up a little bit?"

Chrissey stopped in her foot steps. "It's not cold in here."

"The hell it ain't!" Ebony argued.

"You better grab an electric blanket out the closet cause I'm the only nicca that pay the bills around these parts."

Ebony was just about to cut into Chrissey when the door bell rang.

"Carla get the door, you're the closest." Ebony and Chrissey yelled in unison.

"I mean are y'all going to allow me to pull my pants up, first?" Carla asked sarcastically.

"That's for Joshua to be considerate in that department, not us.'" Chrissey chanted, "Bullseye."

This time it was Carla's turn to flip the bird. When Carla asked who it was, she got a muffled response. Opening the door, she came face to face with Morgan. She wasn't sure if she missed her or if her feelings were still hurt. Before Carla could decide to let Morgan in the house or not, Chrissey appeared over her shoulder.

"Is your petty ass going to unlock the screen?" Chrissey nudged Carla's shoulder.

"It's your house, you do it." Carla relieved Chrissey of the baby and walked back into the living room with him.

Morgan took off her coat and greeted everyone including Carla. "We should talk!"

"And we will talk." Chrissey responded before Carla had the chance. "Right after I finish my story. Sit down Morgan, I was just getting started."

Morgan looked at Carla and then looked at the baby. "He's gorgeous."

"Thank you."

"Can I hold him?" Morgan asked.

Carla hesitated and looked at both of her sisters. Yes, she was petty like that, but decided to be the bigger person. As she got up and handed Morgan the baby, she heard Chrissey say:

"Sothatpettypunkasssonofabitchtriedtoplaymeafteri fuckedhisbrainsoutandmadehimcallhismama…"

UNTIL NEXT TIME LADIES AND GENTLEMEN...

Thank you all for joining me in another journey. This sequel has just advanced into a trilogy! The Williams' girls and I certainly hope that you've enjoyed us. There's more to come and we'll see you next time!

*Turn the page for a snippet
of the next book!*

Marriage

I DO, DON'T I?

I love my husband! He is the apple of my eye; the wind beneath my wings, my eyes when I can not see and the guide when I become weary. My husband is the most considerate when it comes to my needs, receptive of my input, respectful of my feelings and reciprocates my efforts. But, would you like to know the truth? This has not always been the case. After five years of marriage and seven years of being together, there has been growth, destruction, reconstruction, fireworks, explosions, the calm after the storm and the dust after it all has settled.

The misconception about relationships is the happily ever after syndrome that started with the implementation of childhood fairytales. The Little Mermaid, Aladdin, Beauty and the Beast, Princess and the Frog, and Enchanted. There's always a prince charming that comes to save the damsel in distress or the sensual nature of a woman being able to turn the heart of a man. It's all a fairytale, because it's certainly not that easy. In marriage, the plot actually thickens and resolution doesn't come as quickly as a two hour kiddie movie.

The absolute gospel truth is that marriages are more like these movies:

I think I love my wife- where spouses begin to neglect each other and lose sight of why you're with your spouse in the first place. When your attention gets diverted by other people, it opens the door for infidelity.

Baby Boy – Husband and Wives are so irritated and agitated with each other that you're just like Yvette and Jody and you can't figure out if you hate him or love him and vice versa.

Monster-In-Law- The evidence that people will intentionally try to make your life a living hell. They have a need to preserve space in your spouses life without understanding that you are here to add to him/her not take from him/her. The mindset of The Brady Bunch has evaporated and the presence of The Klumps has manipulated the atmosphere.

My marriage was ordained by God, but that doesn't mean that work wasn't required of us. We, as people, unknowingly believe that since God put it together that it should be easy. I remember saying several times, "This should not be this hard! Love doesn't look like this, I can not accept this." But,

I really should have been asking my self these two questions before saying I DO:

1. Am I up for the task?
2. Am I willing to put in the work?

Before you say YES or NO, turn the page!

Printed in the United States
By Bookmasters